S0-DOR-460

Quiz inside: Are you a player?

"Don't you feel guilty at all?"

"Of course I feel bad," I replied to Raina. "I just don't understand why girls freak out so much when I call it quits. I mean, it's not like I'm calling off a serious relationship or anything."

"It's because you're the type of guy girls would *like* to get serious with," Raina explained. She butted her shoulder against mine. "Although why they would want to is a mystery to me."

"Hey!" I said, tugging on her French braid. "You should be happy for me. After all, I'm finally thinking seriously about a girl."

"I am," she said, smiling weakly. "Really. I just hope Trudy is everything you think she is."

Raina was worried about me? For years she'd been on my case about my treatment of girls. Now I was actually focusing on one incredible girl for a change, and Raina was all uneasy?

All That

LYNN MASON

BANTAM BOOKS
NEW YORK · TORONTO · LONDON · SYDNEY · AUCKLAND

For Weezy McDermott. I want to thank the Foster family: Mange, Robyn, Olivia,
and Anna Marie. And special thanks to Rob for believing in me.

RL 6, age 12 and up

ALL THAT

A Bantam Book / August 1999

Cover photography by Michael Segal.

Produced by 17th Street Productions,
a division of Daniel Weiss Associates, Inc.
33 West 17th Street, New York, NY 10011.

ISBN: 0-553-49290-X

Published simultaneously in the United States and Canada

Bantam Books are published by Bantam Books, a division of Random
House, Inc. Its trademark, consisting of the words "Bantam Books" and
the portrayal of a rooster, is Registered in U.S. Patent and Trademark
Office and in other countries. Marca Registrada. Bantam Books, 1540
Broadway, New York, New York 10036.

PRINTED IN THE UNITED STATES OF AMERICA

OPM   0 9 8 7 6 5 4 3 2 1

One

SHELLY ARMSTRONG LOOKED at me, studying my expression to see if I was serious. Suddenly her smooth, round face seemed to crack from all sides. Wavy lines erupted onto her forehead, her mouth bunched up in a scowl, and her nose crinkled up and turned red. Smears of eyeliner and mascara mixed with tears, making her eyes as green and murky as the bayou behind me.

"You . . . you . . . pig!" she shrieked. "Jason Lauderette, you're nothing but a big fat user! I hope you rot!" Her words echoed off the wide outdoor deck of the Scratchin' Post Café, over the trees, and into the swampland beyond. Even the mockingbirds stopped singing.

I know what you're thinking. At this point you're probably guessing that I cheated on this girl or spread horrible, reputation-impairing rumors about her all over town. But all I did was break up with her. I mean, I was being totally honest. I told her it'd been fun, but now it was time to see other people. Then she freaked.

"One of these days *you'll* get treated like spit and you'll get what you deserve!" she hissed. "And when that happens, I'll be laughing!" Shelly's shouts diminished into sobs. She pushed past me and headed toward the café's front entrance.

She probably expected me to run after her and beg forgiveness, but I stood my ground, listening as her cries grew fainter and fainter. I'd discovered that trying to comfort a girl after you've just dumped her is useless. In fact, it only makes things worse. A clean, surgical severing of ties is always the best way to go.

I'd learned a lot about dealing with the opposite sex over the past couple of years. Playing in my band, the Bankheads, gave me the chance to go out with lots of different girls. I used to have a tough time finding the nerve to ask someone out, but performing onstage helped me get cool about it. In fact, *they* usually came up to *me* at shows. I'd talk and flirt with some girl, and before I knew it, I'd be holding a napkin with someone's phone number written on it.

The tough part was figuring out how to keep it casual. For some reason, after a couple of weeks girls would always start referring to "our relationship," wanting me to go fishing with their dads and asking me to open up about my feelings. So far I hadn't figured out the exact point in time when things went from informal to insane. If I could determine that, I could just cut things off right before it happened. Then no one would get upset and make a scene.

Obviously I'd been far too late with Shelly. She threw a final, wretched glance back at me, then retreated through the restaurant's front door, sobbing loudly. I shook my head, let out a sigh of relief, and turned toward my band. The three of them had watched my little melodrama unfold from the safety of the outdoor deck's raised wooden stage. Thankfully, since the café's dinner crowd hadn't shown up yet, they were the only ones who'd witnessed it.

"You're bored with Shelly already?" Raina Baez stood behind her keyboard, her arms crossed against her chest, that all-too-familiar glint of disapproval in her brown eyes. "That's the second girl this month, Jase."

I smiled and rolled my eyes, prepared for Raina to scold me once again for hooking up with too many girls. You see, Raina was my best friend, which gave her the right to get into my business—or at least *she* seemed to think so.

"What am I supposed to do?" I asked, hopping onstage. "You're a girl. You tell me the right way to end things so that no one goes ballistic."

She pointed her long, keyboard-player index finger at me. "Maybe if you didn't end things so *soon,* they wouldn't freak out on you."

I sighed and pulled the strap of my Stratocaster guitar over my head. I knew there was no use arguing with Raina when she thought she was right. She'd been enlightening me with her lectures ever since we'd met in junior-high band class. Back then I was this skinny, squirrelly saxophone player with glasses and a mouth full of metal. Raina was gorgeous (as always) and popular, and she befriended me even though I was of a lower social standing. Of course I had a megacrush on her, but I knew she'd never go out with me. Still, during band class, we discovered that we were a lot alike. Soon we started hanging out after school, talking and throwing rocks into the bayou, or getting together on weekends to watch movies or listen to CDs. At some point—I don't remember when—I got up the nerve to play her some songs I'd written. I expected her to laugh or jab her fingers into my rib cage the way she always did and say, "Keep dreaming, Jase." But instead she encouraged me. She told me my stuff was better than half the junk she heard on the radio. And we even started writing some songs together.

I guess you could say that she was the one who inspired me to go after my dream, as corny as that sounds. But at present, Raina was being nothing more than a royal pain in the butt.

"You get bored way too easily, Jase," Raina continued. "I check out library books for longer than you check out girls."

"Yeah, well, that's because you read slow," I replied with a smirk. "Maybe you should go back to those early-reader books. You know, 'See Dick. See Jane. See Spot run.'"

Raina's left eyebrow rose—as well as the corners of her mouth. "Oh, yeah? How about 'See Jason. See Jason run off at the mouth. See Jason get strangled by a microphone cord'?"

"Enough," Martian called from behind the drum set. Martian's real name is Robert, but everyone has always called him Martian, probably because the guy does look like a visitor from another planet—he's only about five foot five and has these huge eyes that appear even larger through his round eyeglasses. "I already had to watch Shelly yell at Jason," he said. "I don't think my stomach can handle any more ugly scenes."

"You heard the man, Raina," I said with a fake pout. "I've been through enough already."

Raina flashed me a withering look and reached over her keyboard to jab me in the ribs.

"So, Jason. With Shelly gone, who's next in line to be used and abused?" Roscoe, my third bandmate, asked as he plucked out a series of notes on his bass guitar. "You'll have your pick at the show here tonight."

"I bet on Brenda McCoy," Martian put in. "She hasn't missed a gig yet. And *she* is hot."

I rolled my eyes. Did they have nothing better to do than to lay odds on my personal life? "Back off, dudes. I don't need any suggestions," I grumbled, but not before my brain dutifully conjured up images of Brenda in her dance squad uniform. She *was* cute. . . .

Raina must have read my thoughts. "Aw, man,"

she said, gathering her long blond hair up into a ponytail. "Can't you just hold off a couple of weeks? Give yourself a break? At the rate you're going, Tallulah is going to be filled with jilted girls boycotting all our shows. We'll be able to hear the crickets outside between songs."

Roscoe laughed and plucked out a few notes of taps on the bass.

"Wait a minute." I threw up my hands in surrender. "First you're mad because I broke up with Shelly, and now you think I should lay off girls entirely?"

"I just think if you're going to go out with someone, you should continue to see them for a while and really get to know them," Raina explained. "Maybe if you'd hang in there and actually work at having a relationship, you'd see it isn't so bad."

Relationship. There was that word again. Was the phrase "just having a good time" not in the female vocabulary?

"No way, man!" Roscoe shouted. "The worst thing that could happen to this band would be if Jason got serious with a girl and suddenly became unavailable."

"Yeah," Martian echoed. "He's the only reason they come out to see us."

Raina and I glared at him.

"Uh . . . I mean, besides the music," he added.

"Speaking of which, can we *please* get on with this rehearsal?" Raina pleaded. "I want some time for a decent meal before our set tonight."

"Hey, you're the one who's been holding us up," I replied with a wink.

"Me?" Raina put her hands on her hips, her cheeks turning pink. "What about Shelly's little—"

"I know, I know, I'm just kidding," I said with a laugh. I loved it when Raina got all worked up. It was so . . . cute. "All right, guys," I said. "Let's get going."

We finished tuning our instruments, then started one of our newest songs. As I played, the slight annoyance I'd felt over Shelly's outburst and the gang's endless analysis of my social calendar disappeared into the melody. Music always made me feel better, especially when I was the one performing it. For one thing, music made sense. Songs had a pattern, a path, and a clear ending. *They* never asked for a lifelong commitment.

To me, relationships were the same thing as playing the same song over and over forever. Who'd want to do that?

Sylvester mounted the stage and tapped the mike a couple of times. The breeze ruffled his white linen suit, and his gold tooth twinkled like one of the evening stars.

"Welcome to the Scratchin' Post," he said to the crowd. "Y'all ready to rock?"

"Yeah," they responded in unison.

"I said . . . are *y'all* ready to *rock*?" he repeated. *"Yeah!"*

"Naw, naw. Y'all got to do better than that. Say 'Yeah, man.'"

"Yeah, man!"

"Come on now, I want to feel it in my toes. Say *'Yeah, man!'*"

"Yeah, man!"

Good ol' Sylvester. Watching him onstage was like watching an evangelist preach to a choir. He could stir up an audience like wind on dry leaves. Picture Samuel L. Jackson. Now age him twenty years, put a beer belly on him, and give him a gold front tooth. That's Sylvester. The dude was a master musician. He'd been playing blues guitar since his diaper days, but he'd taken some time off recently because of the arthritis in his fingers.

Twenty years ago he opened up the Scratchin' Post Café. By day it was a restaurant, offering spicy Cajun cuisine and a great view of the bayou. But Thursday, Friday, and Saturday nights at eight o'clock, it was *the* place to be to hear live music. For years Raina and I would come hang out and listen to local bluegrass musicians, blues guitarists, or zydeco bands perform on the big wooden deck, and we got to know Sylvester pretty well.

That spring, before the end of school, Sylvester had really come through for us. He told me and Raina that he wanted to hire a band to play regularly on Saturday nights. Most of his blues buddies preferred the Thursday or Friday spots, so that their weekends were free for family and church activities. Sylvester asked if we'd like to audition for the slot. I could've kissed him. After years of playing parties for free, now we actually had a chance to do paid gigs. So one afternoon after school we lugged down our equipment, which we painstakingly set up and tuned, and played him two of our best songs.

"You know what you are, sonny?" he'd said to me after we'd finished. "You're a diamond. You're a little rough around the edges, but still a diamond. And there's nothing like a weekly gig to smooth out them rough spots. You boys—and lady—have got yourself a job."

Not exactly a *People* magazine success story, but we felt as though we had it made. Now we could play on a *real* stage, use Sylvester's *real* sound equipment, and earn *real* money—well, 20 percent of the food and drink profits, plus whatever ended up in the tip jar, but at least it was something.

"Say 'Gimme some Bankheads!'" Sylvester continued whipping up the crowd.

"Gimme some Bankheads!" they echoed.

"I said the beboppin' ho-dee-poppin' Bankheads!"

"Beboppa . . ." *mumble mumble* ". . . Bankheads!" they attempted.

"Uh-huh!"

"Uh-huh!"

"I wish he wouldn't build us up like this," Raina whispered to me offstage. "I feel so undeserving."

"He knows what he's doing," I told her. But I knew what she meant. Sylvester's intro was making my palms sweat too.

"All right now," said Sylvester, holding up a hand as if he were yielding to the crowd. "Y'all get your wish. Ladies and gentlemen, put your hands together for the Bankheads!" Sylvester gave us our cue and gestured for us to emerge.

He'd really done a number on the audience. As we walked onstage and took up our instruments, the air reverberated with applause, whistles, and girls' squeals. Raina muttered something to me, but I couldn't catch it. My ears were too busy registering all the noise in the place, generated by my presence.

"Thank you," I said into the mike. As I slung my guitar over my head and checked the tuning, my eyes wandered over the crowd, estimating its size. Brenda McCoy, looking incredible in some sort of lacy top, waved at me from the right side of the deck. Behind me Raina cleared her throat in supposed preparation for her backup vocals, but I knew it was also her subtle way of sending me a message.

We started into our first number, a pop tune that Raina and I had written a year earlier, called "Killing Time." It was mainly about being bored on a Sunday afternoon, but everyone seemed to think it was a love song, especially the part that goes, "Let's get together and do something new / Without you I'd have nothing to do." When I got to those lines, Brenda gestured toward me and mouthed along with the words. I watched her all through the next verse and the one after that as she twisted along to the rhythm in a sexy sort of dance.

Maybe I will *ask her out,* I thought. *She seems pretty cool.*

But then, as we started our next song, a cover of the Smashing Pumpkins' "1979," I noticed Kimmy Dangerfield in the front row, on the opposite end from where Brenda stood. For two weeks she had missed our gigs since she'd gone on a family vacation to Hawaii. Now she was back in town, sporting a caramel-colored tan and a flowered wraparound dress. She looked gorgeous—and she was staring right at me.

For the rest of the song I couldn't help but check out both Brenda and Kimmy. I'd face left and get some winning smiles from Kimmy, then pivot to the right and see Brenda doing her flirty dance. It was such a trip—as if I were some big rock star or something. *Turn and watch Kimmy. Turn and watch Brenda. Repeat.* By the time I hit the final chord I needed to rest. I turned my back to the audience and grabbed a few swigs from Raina's water bottle.

"Will you please just choose one of those two bookends and get on with it?" Raina whispered, her hand covering the microphone. "I'm getting dizzy just watching you."

"I don't know what you're talking about," I lied. I hadn't realized my fun with Kimmy and Brenda had been so obvious. But what guy in my position wouldn't do the same thing?

Raina narrowed her eyes. "Jase, you're going to get yourself in trouble."

11

Jeez, I thought. Raina could never cut me a break. "Isn't there something you're supposed to be doing now?" I asked, scratching my head and pretending to look confused. "Like playing your synthesizer? Would you mind terribly if I go back to doing our gig?"

She rolled her eyes and placed her hands on the keyboard. "Just watch it, all right?" she muttered.

Our next number was a real pumped-up funk tune I'd written two years before, back when I'd gone through a Red Hot Chili Peppers phase. The song always got people moving on the dance floor. Plus it was Roscoe's chance to show off. I swear, the dude got so carried away onstage, sometimes we'd have to prevent him from smashing up equipment just for the thrill of it.

I stood there under the stage lights, crooning into the microphone and taking in every detail of the scene. The guitar felt alive in my grasp—an extra limb I could control as naturally and effortlessly as breathing. Beside me, tall and skinny Roscoe hopped up and down in some sort of crazed jump-rope-champion routine. And in front of us, the crowd surged and undulated like a colorful amoeba. I was in the zone. Everything was perfect.

Well . . . almost. The chorus was making me cringe despite myself. And the transitions sounded too stiff. In fact, the harder I listened, the worse it all sounded.

Party pooper, I grumbled to myself.

It was the same as always. Whenever we'd perform, the music just didn't come off exactly right to me, and I wasn't sure why. The other band members always said I was a major perfectionist, but it was more than that. I could tell our songs were lacking something. Even when we'd hit every note and the audience would go wild, the impact was never quite the way I'd imagined it. It was always slightly wrong—like a picture hanging a few millimeters off center.

That night's set was no exception. As incredible as the crowd's energy was, I still sensed there was something a bit crooked with our music.

We finished the song, and everyone cheered. Brenda hopped up and down. Kimmy raised her bronzed arms and clapped over her head.

See? It couldn't have been that bad, I told myself. *Everyone's totally into it.*

Or almost *everyone.*

As I scanned the room, I spotted someone in back who wasn't clapping—a gorgeous girl I'd never seen before. She definitely was not from Tallulah. Her dress looked kind of sophisticated for the café—a few jumps up the scale from the shorts and halters that were all the rage in my town. And her hair was cut short and sleek. Most girls in Tallulah liked their hair as long and curly as possible. Plus, while everyone else was dancing, whistling, and having a total blast, she was casually leaning against the bar and sipping her iced tea, looking like a queen surveying her kingdom.

I couldn't take my eyes off her. She was far more beautiful than any other girl I'd ever seen in person.

For a second I wondered if she was a model or something. And I could tell the girl had attitude by the way she acted—as if *she* were the star attraction there that night instead of us.

Suddenly the mystery girl seemed to pick up my frequency and glanced in my direction. The instant our eyes locked, a jolt of energy surged through me, as if I'd been zapped by some sort of phaser. I nearly forgot the lyrics in midverse. Still, I managed a cool smile.

She smiled back.

For the rest of the set she watched me, seemingly interested, yet she never approached the stage. She just remained at the bar, rattling the ice in her drink and looking as sleek and mysterious as a stretch limousine. I knew I had to meet her.

I vaguely remember playing our last three songs. Then, finally, our set was over. I thanked the audience, took off my guitar, and quickly stepped off the stage, aiming for the back of the room. But as soon as I took a step in the mystery girl's direction I became surrounded by fans. Brenda and her friends came at me from the right, while Kimmy and her group swarmed in from the left.

"Jason! You were so great tonight."

"I just love the way your face scrunches up during that guitar solo."

"Can I grab you a drink of water? You look so . . . hot."

Normally I'd be eating up their comments like Halloween candy, but this time I was in a hurry to

14

get past them. I ran the back of my hand over my sweaty forehead and smiled politely. "Thanks. Thanks a lot. Glad you enjoyed the show. If you ladies will pardon me a sec, there's someone I need to talk to."

Flashing an apologetic look, I sidestepped through the group and resumed my original trajectory toward the front counter. Only I was too late.

On top of the bar sat an empty iced tea tumbler with a red circle of lipstick on the rim. But the unknown superbabe was nowhere in sight.

Two

"YOU KNOW, I'VE been thinking," Roscoe told us.

"No kidding? You?" Martian quipped.

"Wow! I'll call the local paper!" Raina exclaimed.

"Did it hurt?" I asked, unable to resist.

"Come on, guys. Lay off. This is serious." Roscoe slumped back in his chair, frowning down at his food.

It was the day after the gig and we were all sitting in the Scratchin' Post, enjoying the day's special. For two straight summers Raina had worked as a part-time waitress—which translated into free food and drink for me, Martian, and Roscoe. Raina had some time before her shift started, and the rest of us were taking advantage of the free-lunch benefit.

"All right. I'll bite," I said to Roscoe. "What have you been thinking?"

He sat forward quickly and grinned excitedly. "Okay. I was watching MTV today, and I think I know how we can get famous."

Raina flashed me a wary look. Roscoe was always coming up with these ridiculous schemes to get us noticed by record agents or talent scouts.

"Roscoe, if you mean that crazy idea of having me dress up like Xena the Warrior Princess, you can forget it," Raina said.

"No, no. It's not anything stupid."

"Good," Martian, Raina, and I all said in unison.

"No, what I'm talking about is simple, really. I think we should change our names. They just aren't rock-and-roll enough."

"What do you mean?" Raina asked, wrinkling up her eyebrows.

"Think about it. Jason Lauderette, Raina Baez, Roscoe Cunningham. All our names are pretty boring—no offense. The only one with the cool name is Martian."

"But I *hate* being called that," Martian whined.

Roscoe ignored him. "I figure if we each went by a wild nickname, it would make us more, you know, marketable or whatever."

Raina nodded slowly. "Uh-huh. So what exactly do you think we should name ourselves?"

"I thought we could each think of something that describes us—the way Martian's name describes him."

"Hey!" Martian grumbled.

"Jason could be Studmaster J," Roscoe continued.

"Oh, no," I laughed. "No way, man."

Roscoe pointed at Raina. "And you should go by something sexy. Something along the lines of Ginger Spice or Xena the Warrior Princess."

"All right! That does it! Of all the—"

I cut Raina off in the middle of her rant. "And what do *you* want to be called, Roscoe?"

He leaned forward across the table and lowered his voice. "Guys, from now on I want you to call me . . . Claw."

For a second or two we just blinked back at him, collectively processing his words. Then Martian pushed back his chair. "That's it," he declared dramatically. "I'm finding a new band."

A cacophony of bickering welled up at the table. Raina told Roscoe that he should watch less MTV and practice more, Roscoe listed rock stars with weird names, and Martian complained that he didn't want people to call him Martian anymore.

I sensed it was time for someone to take charge. "Okay. Okay. Enough!" I hollered over the din. "Martian, you aren't going anywhere. And Roscoe— sorry, man, but we're not changing our names. Now, can we please focus on some real business? There just so happens to be an opportunity coming up that could give us a real break."

"Oh, yeah? What's that?" Roscoe asked sullenly.

"Fourthfest," I replied, slapping my palm on the table. "We have less than a week to get a demo to the judges."

Every Fourth of July, Tallulah hosted a big

outdoor music festival called Fourthfest. It was held on a huge farm just outside of town and featured music from all over Louisiana, and even beyond. Lately it had attracted some big-name bands, but its main purpose was to showcase lesser-known native musicians. A panel of judges would listen to all the demo tapes they'd been sent and would then book the top ten acts. The year before, we hadn't made it, but I knew we had a relatively good chance that summer—if we ever got our tape finished.

"Aw, man. There's no way," Martian whined. "We might as well try out for the Horde tour."

"We have to at least try," Raina said.

"Exactly." I smiled at her, and she grinned back. Finally, some band unity. "So. Can you guys come over to my house tonight to rehearse?"

Raina nodded. "I'm there."

"Yeah, whatever," Martian said.

"Okay," Roscoe mumbled.

"Come on, guys. Where's your spirit? We're going to make it this year for sure!" I prompted. "Hey, we ruled the place last night, didn't we?"

That got them. Soon they were all talking about how tight our gig had sounded and how worked up the crowd had been. It really had been a good show: great audience, high energy, no big mistakes. From all outward appearances, we had the stuff to make it. Yet I still couldn't shake that nagging sense that something wasn't exactly right.

No way was I going to tell them that, though. If

we were going to have a shot at Fourthfest, I had to keep them fired up. Nothing could kill a band faster than a loss of attitude.

"Well, it's been real, dudes," Roscoe told us, "but it's time for me to take off." He rose from his chair, and with a dramatic salute he turned and walked off.

"Yeah. Me too," Martian said. "See you guys tonight." He trotted after Roscoe's disappearing shadow.

"Bye, Martian," I called out. "Bye . . . Claw."

Raina laughed. Then she leaned toward me, an amused sparkle in her deep-set brown eyes. "I noticed you didn't hang out with any of the groupies after the show, Jase," she said. "Does that mean you've decided to take my advice after all and give things a rest?"

"Hmmm. Now why exactly do you think I should hold off the girls for a while?" I asked, rubbing my chin.

Raina pursed her lips. She hated it when I answered her questions with a question. "Because." She sighed. "You're a jerk."

I chuckled. Raina was never one to beat around the bush. "No, really, Rain. Tell it to me straight. I can handle it."

She shook her head and stared down at the tabletop. "I mean it. You're always leading all those girls on."

"What are you talking about? All I do is have fun with them. Nothing heavy. *They* always bring up the stuff about having a relationship."

21

"My point exactly. These girls have feelings for you, and you take advantage of them." She sat back in her chair and folded her arms across her chest. "Do you remember what your social life was like back in junior high?"

"Uh . . . would that be the nonexistent social life or the imaginary one?" I asked with a smirk. "Come on, Rain, you were there. I couldn't get a girl if they were on sale at Wal-Mart."

"Right!" Raina exclaimed, pointing her finger at me like a lawyer pouncing on a witness. "You, of all people, should remember what it's like to get blown off."

"Huh. Have you ever stopped to think that since I was such a dweeb in junior high, I have the right to, you know, make up for lost time?"

Raina kicked me under the table. "I'm serious!"

"Me too. Look, Rain, I appreciate the pep talk and all, but I'm not the force of evil you're making me out to be." I leaned forward and shot her a disarming puppy-dog expression. "Come on, you can say it. Repeat after me. 'Jason is not the Antichrist.'"

Her frown quivered for a couple of seconds before curling upward. Then she rolled her eyes and giggled. "All right, all right. I'm sorry to stick my nose in your business all the time. But seriously, I was glad you showed some restraint last night and resisted the girls."

"Well . . ." I ducked my head sheepishly. "There *was* this one girl I wanted to hook up with more than anything. Man, was she hot!"

Raina's smile disappeared. "Really? What girl?"

"The one in back by the bar. Short dark hair, great body, wearing a black dress?"

"It was probably Angie Craven," Raina said. "She got her hair cut kind of short recently."

"No, no. This was no one I'd ever seen before. The girl is definitely from out of town. I was hoping to meet her, but she left before our set ended."

Raina reached over and placed her hand on my forehead. "You sure you weren't daydreaming about Neve Campbell?"

"No! You really don't know who I'm talking about? You didn't see the girl at all?"

She shrugged. "Sorry. I was sort of busy, you know. Playing our gig and all."

I ran a hand through my shaggy hair. How could Raina not have noticed her? To me she had seemed to light up the room like an exploding star. Had I only been hallucinating, as Raina suggested? Maybe I did need to lay off females for a while.

"Well, I'd love to stay and psychoanalyze these imaginary women you're seeing, but I'm late for my shift." Raina stood and grabbed her apron off the back of her chair. "You want me to bring you some more tea?"

"Huh?" I said distractedly. I was still thinking about my mystery girl, wondering if I'd ever see her again—if she existed, that is. "Uh, no. No, thanks."

"You all right?"

"Yeah. I was just thinking."

"Be careful when you do that. You see where it gets Roscoe," Raina said, flashing me a wry grin. She punched me lightly on my shoulder, then bounced off toward the kitchen.

I pushed the remaining bits of gumbo around in my bowl, conjuring up the image of the dark-haired beauty from the night before. I'd felt an overwhelming need to know her, as if she'd been sent straight to me—a gift from the gods. But I guessed it just wasn't meant to be. She was probably just a tourist stopping off I-20 on her way to Dallas. I'd most likely never see her again.

The realization made my heart twinge.

"Well, well, lookee here. If it isn't Jason Lauderette." Sylvester loomed over my table like the Statue of Liberty, a tray of dirty dishes balanced high in his hand. "You come to eat my food or take another bow onstage?"

"Today I'm here for the gumbo, and *you're* the one who should be taking a bow. It's delicious."

He chuckled and took a seat across from me, setting the tray down on a nearby empty table. "That was some show last night. You people have been practicing hard, I see."

I felt my heart twinge again. "Um, yeah, it was cool," I replied, trying to sound convincing. "The crowd sure seemed into it."

"You got that right," he said with a wink.

I exhaled slowly, drumming my fingers on the

rim of my plate. I had to figure out some way to improve my music or I'd go nuts. It was totally exasperating to want something so badly, work at it so hard, and always come up a few yards short. "Sylvester, can I ask you something?"

"Shoot."

"Do you think we're good enough to get into Fourthfest?"

He smiled diplomatically. "Well, now, I don't know about that. But you won't know unless you try, will you?"

I looked down at Sylvester's large hands. His nails were split at the ends, and his fingers looked rough and callused. The marks of a true guitar player.

"Tell me the truth," I said, meeting his eyes directly. "What does my music need? What's missing?"

For a few seconds he just studied my gaze, nodding slowly as if I were answering a question instead of asking one. Then he grinned and shook his head. "All right. I'll tell you what I think."

"Thanks," I said. "I could really use the advice."

"You know, son," he began, settling back in his chair, "your playing is good technically. You got the moves, you got the rhythm, and you got some nice, catchy hooks. The only thing missing is soul."

"Soul?" I repeated.

"That's right. Here, let me explain. Sit back, close your eyes, and think about the greatest music you've heard," he said.

"Uh . . . okay," I said, following Sylvester's instructions.

"Can you hear it?"

"Yeah," I replied, nodding along to the Rolling Stones' "You Can't Always Get What You Want."

"Good. Now think for a minute about what makes it great," Sylvester continued. "Chances are it ain't about guitar chords or meter. It's about the way it *moves* you. You see, it's not enough for your songs to rock—they've got to bleed, they've got to cry, they've even got to laugh sometimes."

I nodded slowly. I knew what he meant, sort of. He was right. There was music out there that I could admire from a purely technical point of view. And then there were songs that might not be all that showy but could reduce people to big quivering piles of emotion. That was what separated the good from the great. That was what I wanted to be.

"I can do that, Sylvester. I'm sure I can. Could you show me how?"

Sylvester threw his head back and laughed. "That ain't nothing you can learn. That something's got to come from inside. From here." He reached over and thumped me lightly on my chest.

"But maybe if I just work harder at—"

"Son, maybe you work too hard," he said, shaking a finger at me. "Maybe you need to stop focusing on your music so much and start focusing on life. Then you can really sing about it." He got up from his chair and picked his tray back up. "Now, if you'll excuse me, there are some customers I need to feed."

"Thanks, Sylvester," I called out as he slowly ambled off.

Sometimes when Sylvester answered my questions I ended up more confused than ever.

After I left the Scratchin' Post, I decided to walk down a couple of blocks to the music store. I'd managed to mooch a few bucks off my mom that morning, and I was in dire need of new guitar strings.

I was walking alongside Grant's Canal, trying to decipher Sylvester's advice, when who should I see pedaling down the street in front of me but the longest, shapeliest legs in all of Tallulah—Darcy Satterwhite's!

Darcy was this wholesomely pretty, Jewel–meets–Mother Earth kind of girl who was known for bicycling around town (she was completely against car exhaust fumes), distributing Greenpeace flyers, and getting people to sign all sorts of environmental petitions. All her riding around really was great for the local scenery in one sense: Darcy, by unanimous vote, was considered to have the best legs in town. For years I'd been wanting to meet her. But she went to a different school, Tallulah Academy, and didn't hang out at our gigs.

As I watched her coast down the road toward me, I suddenly caught her eye. I smiled and lifted my hand in a wave. She waved back and braked to a stop.

27

"Hi there," she said. "Would you like to sign a petition to save the gray whales' breeding ground?" She pulled a clipboard and a pen from her backpack and held them out to me.

I shrugged. "Sure. Do you find many people who are against gray whales breeding?"

"No," she replied, grinning, "but a lot of people don't realize that a major auto manufacturer wants to build a factory right next to the whales' refuge. When you think about the animals' point of view, it helps a lot. I mean, how would you like having a polluting smokestack in your bedroom?"

I took the clipboard from her hands and signed my name on one of the blank lines. "Actually, there might be one. I don't know. I haven't had time to clean my room lately."

Darcy laughed and shook her head. Reddish strands that had fallen from her braid danced captivatingly around her face.

"I'm Jason, by the way. Jason Lauderette." I gave back her clipboard and held out my hand.

"I know," she replied shyly. She quickly stuffed her things in her pack and grasped my palm firmly. "I saw your band play at a party last year. My name's Darcy. Darcy Satterwhite."

"I know," I said, smiling.

Darcy beamed bashfully, the tops of her cheeks coloring to the exact strawberry hue as her hair.

"So . . ." She took her hand from mine, looking a little uncertain. "I really like your music."

"Thanks," I replied.

"Well, I probably should get going." Darcy turned the front wheel of her bike toward the street but let her gaze linger on me. "Do you know anyone else who might want to sign my petition . . . like your girlfriend, maybe?"

I shook my head. "Can't help you there. I don't have a girlfriend."

Her smile seemed to widen. "Oh—okay. I mean, I'm sure I'll still get lots of signatures." She nervously tapped her toe against the street. "Anyway, I guess I'll see you around."

"Sure thing," I replied. Then I had a thought. "Actually, there's another charitable cause you could help me out with. A certain matter of a starving musician. How would you like to have lunch with me?"

Darcy's eyes widened as she blushed again. "Oh! I'm sorry. . . ." She shifted her weight on her long, lovely legs and shrugged helplessly. "I'm actually on my way to a baby-sitting job right now. But how about later on this week?"

"Sure," I said. "I'll call you tonight, okay?"

"Okay. We're the only Satterwhites in the book." She grinned. Then, with a sweet wave and a push of those amazing legs, she disappeared down the block.

He scores! I watched until Darcy's braid disappeared around a corner, then resumed my walk to the music store. *Jason, my man, today must be your lucky day.*

"Nice job," came a voice from behind me.

I spun around.

There, standing in the doorway of Napoleon's Books and CDs, was the beautiful mystery girl from the night before. I wondered if I was fully conscious, or if everything that had occurred after leaving the café had been a Cajun-spice-induced dream.

"You're smooth," she continued, a small smile on her lips. "Do you usually work that fast?"

"Uh . . ." was all I could say.

"Well, you *were* smooth." She raised one eyebrow, and her greenish eyes glittered.

"You . . . you were at the Scratchin' Post last night," I pointed out rather stupidly. "But you left right after the show."

The girl gazed past me down the street. She fiddled with a sleek-looking, thick silver bracelet on her left wrist. "Yeah, well, I was tired and wanted to go home. I'd just driven into town a couple of hours earlier."

"Really?" Speech was coming more easily now. I took a few steps toward her and leaned against a lamppost, trying to look cool. "How long are you in Tallulah for?"

"Three weeks," she said, her face falling. "My mother got remarried recently and is honeymooning in Europe. She wanted me to stay with my aunt and uncle instead of staying home alone. Like I'm not able to take care of myself."

"Where's home?" I asked.

"New Orleans."

"Ah . . . ," I said, as if everything made sense now. She did have that worldly, ultrahip air about her that I associated with New Orleans. Probably knew good music when she heard it too. "So . . . what did you think of our gig last night?"

She lifted her shoulders noncommittally. "It was fun. Pop isn't the big thing at my school, but my cousin says you guys are hot stuff around here."

"Oh." I decided to count her comments as a favorable review. "Who's your cousin?"

"Arlene Balzen. Do you know her?"

Arlene was this supercute, petite girl—one of the school's star gymnasts. She was always smiling and laughing, and had a sense of humor that was rivaled only by Raina's.

"Arlene? Yeah, I know her. Nice girl. Is your name Balzen too?"

"Me?" She seemed amused at the thought. "No. My name is Neidhart. Trudy Neidhart."

She didn't offer her hand, but I grabbed it up anyway. Her skin was silky soft and her nails were perfectly polished. On her third finger she wore a ring with a gigantic dark blue stone in it. I hoped it wasn't a gift from a serious boyfriend.

"I'm Jason. Jason Lauderette."

Since Arlene had talked to her about our band, I half expected her to say, "I know." Instead she replied, "Nice to meet you," and smiled at me, revealing a row of perfectly straight, perfectly white teeth. I marveled at how everything about her seemed flawless. Not even a hair out of place.

"Pleasure's mine." I squeezed her hand, reluctant to let go. "How'd you like to join me for a soda?" I asked her. "My treat." I still held her right hand, and I transferred it to my left, preparing to steer her across the street to Brock's Pharmacy's soda fountain. "Then afterward maybe I could take you on a brief tour of the town?"

Trudy slipped her hand from mine. "Thanks anyway, but I think I already have plans."

"Oh . . . okay." Her unenthusiastic response threw me off a little. I could have sworn she was into me. "So, what's the Balzens' phone number? I could call you tonight and we could set up something else."

Trudy studied me for a moment, a curious glint in her green eyes. "I'll tell you what. How about you give me your phone number?"

"Me?" That was a new one. "Uh, sure."

She produced a pen and a slip of paper from her expensive-looking leather bag, and I dutifully scrawled down my seven digits.

"Great," she said, snatching the paper from my hand. "Maybe I'll call you sometime."

Then, before I could say anything, she walked to a nearby fire-engine-red sports car and drove off, waving at me with the hand that held my number.

I'd never felt so surprised by a girl's actions before—and I loved it. Instead of openly flirting and dropping unmistakable hints that she liked me, Trudy was more . . . subtle and classy. First she turned me down flat when I asked her out, then she asked for my number—that had *never* happened to me before. I just couldn't read her.

But I did know one thing: I had to see her again. It might take a little extra effort to land Trudy, but she'd definitely be worth it.

Finally, a challenge I could enjoy.

Three

"OKAY, NOW. FROM the top. And a one, and a two, and a . . ."

We jumped into the song. The intro sounded great—good timing, good mix, just the right buildup, and then . . . *screech, rumble, crash, squeak* . . . the momentum disappeared and the melody disintegrated into a sea of noise.

"*Aaugh!*" I hollered. "What's going on? Why can't we hold it together?"

Everyone immediately everyone started to point at everyone else.

"Raina's too loud."

"Roscoe's too fast."

"Martian's slowing me down."

I wondered if Dave Matthews ever had these problems with his band, or if the Beastie Boys bickered as much as we did. Here I'd called an emergency rehearsal to record a tape for the Fourthfest judges, and we couldn't even work through the first song.

"Guys, let's try it again," I said. "This time stick to the rhythm. And a one, and a two, and a . . ."

Again we started off great. Then midway through the chorus we began sounding like a group of terrified farm animals.

"All right! Stop! Cut!" I shouted. Gradually the unbearable racket sputtered, whimpered, and died. I spun around and leaned over the drum set. "Martian! Stop adding all those fancy fills. We're not Metallica."

"Aw, man. It's so boring the way you want it," Martian whined.

"And Roscoe," I added, turning back around, "you're hitting the wrong beats. It's not supposed to go *ba, ba, boom, ba, ba, boom*. Listen—it goes *boom, ba, ba, ba, boom, ba, ba, ba*."

"Can we stop with all the *boom*s and *bam*s for a minute?" My mother's head poked through the doorway to the garage. "Your father is trying to watch the news."

"But Mom," I protested, "we've got to finish this demo tape!"

"Well, I'm sure that's very important—whatever it is—but your father has a headache. Maybe you could, you know, take five?"

Mom was always trying to understand the teen music scene, but she really had no clue. She constantly messed up band names, referring to "Mashed Pumpkin" or the "Main Street Boys."

Once when I mentioned Marilyn Manson, Mom asked, "Is she that pretty singer who never shaves under her arms?"

"Okay," I said with a defeated sigh. "I guess we could use a short break. But we really need to start up again after the news and record this song. We're trying for Fourthfest again."

"Are you?" she asked excitedly. "Cool beans!"

I winced. I wished Mom wouldn't use that phrase. It was so mid-90s.

"Well, all right, honey. The news will be over in about twenty minutes. By then I'm sure your father will feel better. Besides, your practice can't go on too late, you know. Or old Mrs. Sapp will call nine-one-one again."

My bandmates and I put down our instruments and headed out into the sultry evening air. We sprawled out on the grass in the shape of a giant X, with our heads together at the center. For a while we just lay there quietly, swatting mosquitoes and looking up at the clouds—wispy threads of white, like brushed cotton. Pollen from a nearby pecan tree spiced the air, and the intermingling chirps of birds and locusts provided a soothing background music.

I was bummed. Everything was going haywire. We couldn't get our music right, and no amount of practicing seemed to help. How were we going to make it into Fourthfest—and beyond—if we couldn't get this soul thing worked out?

And then there was Trudy. I hadn't been so nervous around a girl since junior high. For some reason she put me on edge. And that just made me want to go out with her more.

I closed my eyes and let the soft, hushing sounds of nature sweep away my thoughts. Nothing like a humid Tallulah evening to clear your head. "So, gang," I murmured after a while, "what stops should we make when we go on our world tour? Rome? Paris?"

There was a brief silence, and then Roscoe jumped into the game. "I think Stockholm has a cool music scene. Definitely there. And Berlin is supposed to be a party city."

"And London will provide lots of great shots for the camera crew that's following us around, filming our rockumentary," Raina added. "You know, Roscoe making faces at the palace guards. Martian chasing pigeons in Trafalgar Square."

Every now and then we'd do this—plan what we were going to do when we were famous. We'd choose which bands we'd like to go on tour with, whose movies we'd want to do sound tracks for, and what we would wear to the MTV Video Awards.

"You know what would be totally cool?" Martian asked. "I'd like to be a guest voice on *South Park,* or maybe *Space Ghost Coast to Coast.*"

"I want to buy a huge mansion . . ."

"It'll have to be huge for you to fit in it, Roscoe," Raina commented.

". . . and put a refrigerator in every room. That way I won't have to walk very far to get a snack."

"My house will have one of those flat TV screens that fill up a whole wall!" Martian exclaimed, opening his arms wide. "Sarah Michelle Gellar's cleavage will be as big as me."

"I'd like a private place in the Rocky Mountains. Or maybe along the Pacific coast somewhere." Raina sighed happily.

"What about you, Jason? What will be in your dream house?" Roscoe asked.

I shrugged. "I don't know. It would be cool to have my own studio."

"And lots of secret exits so you can hide all your girlfriends from each other," Roscoe teased.

"Yeah, right," I chuckled.

"Face it, dude," Roscoe said. "You're going to be, like, a heartthrob. One of *People* magazine's sexiest humans. Your face will be in those 'Hunks of America' calendars and taped to the insides of girls' lockers."

"His face is already taped up in girls' lockers," Martian muttered.

Suddenly the game wasn't fun anymore. "You guys just don't get it," I said, sitting up. "You think I play music only to get girls?"

Martian and Roscoe scrambled to a sitting position and exchanged puzzled glances. "Yeah," Roscoe replied. "I mean, doesn't everyone?"

"No. *I* don't," I said.

"Yes, you do," Martian said, shaking his finger at me.

"No! I don't," I insisted. I couldn't believe they

would think I was that shallow. First Sylvester said I was lacking soul, and now this. How could I make people understand how much my music mattered to me?

"I know how we can settle this." Roscoe leaned over Raina's sprawled form. "Raina, set this boy straight. He's doing the music thing just to meet the ladies, isn't he?"

Oh, great, I thought. *Now I'm fried.* All that day needed was a lengthy lecture from Raina about how I was such a jerk with girls.

Raina sat up slowly, picked a couple of twigs out of her thick blond hair, and turned to face us. "No," she said calmly. "He isn't."

My mouth fell open. Her response was not at all what I'd expected.

"But . . . but you're always on his case!" Roscoe protested. "You say he takes advantage of the groupies!"

"He does," she said, nodding. "But that's *not* why he plays music. Jason plays music because he has to. It's just who he is."

While Martian and Roscoe voiced their objections and accused us of conspiring together, Raina and I exchanged small smiles.

Her words echoed through me, lightening my mood. *Who he is. . . .* She was right. I couldn't have said it better.

That's my best friend, I thought, shaking my head in amazement. *Sometimes she knows me better than I know myself.*

*   *   *

Three hours later we finally taped a decent two-song demo. Actually, it sounded pretty great considering all the fighting that went on. But that's how a band works. You butt heads, you give in a little, and then you end up finding a groove everyone is satisfied with—except for me, as usual, with my inability to experience real satisfaction with anything we did. I only hoped the judges liked it enough to consider us.

"Jase, we're in for sure. I have a really good feeling." Raina sat slouched against a speaker, watching the moths dance around the lamppost in the driveway. Roscoe and Martian had gone home, and Raina and I were having our usual postpractice hangout session.

"Yeah. I do too. Sort of. There's just one thing that bothers me." I flopped down next to her and sighed.

"What's that?"

"Sylvester says my music doesn't have any soul."

"Soul?" she repeated, stretching out the word.

"Yeah, you know. Our songs should . . . move people."

She nudged me playfully. "Hey, they move. I see people dancing all the time."

"I mean they should affect them emotionally," I told her.

Raina laughed. "Judging by your social calendar, I'd say *you* affect them emotionally."

"Come on, Rain. You know what I'm trying to say," I mumbled. "Don't start in on me like Martian and Roscoe."

"Look," Raina said, tilting her head toward me and placing her hand on my arm. "You just turned eighteen and your band already has a regular gig at the hottest spot in town. I'd say you're doing great."

"But I want to do more."

"I know, but jeez! Have some patience. Musicians whose careers peak before they turn twenty are usually broke and robbing liquor stores by the age of thirty-five."

I smiled. "Scary thought. But I can almost see Roscoe enjoying that."

We laughed, then sat silently for a moment, watching the moths perform their death-defying ballet around the sizzling yellow lightbulb.

"It'll happen, Jase," Raina said, bumping up against me with her shoulder. "Every day you learn more and get a little better. You have the rest of your life to work on getting soul."

I shrugged weakly. "Yeah. I guess you're right."

"Damn straight. I'm always right," she said, whacking me on the kneecap. "Hey, maybe we can go to the Scratchin' Post on Friday night and watch the old blues guitarists do their stuff. You can take a few notes while we're there."

"Um . . . I can't. I think I'll have a date that night."

"Oh, really? With who?"

"Well, it'll be with either Darcy Satterwhite or this other girl I met today." I knew that would bother her, but it was the truth. Besides, I could never keep anything from Raina.

"What?" Raina's brown eyes practically jumped from her lids. "You have two girls lined up? Jase!"

"No, it's not like that. I met Darcy and asked her out, but then I ran into my mystery girl and asked her out." I cleared my throat and ran a hand through my hair. "Only, uh, she said no."

"She said no?" Raina broke into a smile. "Who *is* this girl?"

"Her name's Trudy. She's from New Orleans. And before you start truly enjoying the fact that she turned me down, you should know that she did ask for my phone number and said she'd call me sometime soon."

"*She* asked *you?* Hmmm. Interesting."

"Anyway." My voice rose somewhat. The smug look on Raina's face was starting to get to me. "I'll make plans with Darcy, but I'll rearrange things if Trudy calls and says she can go out. Darcy's cool and all, but this girl is . . . I don't know, very different. Special."

"She sounds different, all right." Raina nodded. "But if you want my advice, which I'm sure you don't, it sounds like this whole thing will explode in your face—and you don't want to get burned."

I grinned impishly. "Hey, you know me. I like things hot. Hot weather, hot food, hot women . . ."

"Ugh! Spare me!" Raina raised her hand between us. Then she suddenly looked at her watch and bounced to her feet. "Oops! Didn't realize it was so late. I'd better pack up my keyboard and get going."

"Here," I said, standing. "Let me help you lift it into the case."

"No, I can handle it," she insisted. "I'm not some china doll, you know."

I think hanging out with three guys for so long had made Raina ultradefensive about being a female. She couldn't stand it if we helped her carry stuff or held doors for her.

"Come on, Rain," I said, watching her struggle with the bulky synthesizer. "I'm always lugging stuff for Martian. And I let Roscoe help me unload all the time. Why can't I just give you a hand?"

"Because I say so," she said in a sugar-sweet voice, looking up at me with a hint of playfulness in her eyes. Then she carefully lowered the keyboard into its case, slammed the cover shut, and stood up triumphantly.

"Oh, tough girl, huh?" I teased, punching her gently on the shoulder.

She countered with a light jab to my chin. "You bet."

"All right, let's see what you've got, Baez," I said, dancing around like a prizefighter. I held my left arm up to block and punched the air with my right. "Come on, show me your best moves."

"You asked for it," she drawled, circling me cautiously, arms ready for attack.

I cupped my hands over my mouth and called out in my best ring-announcer voice, "Let's get ready to *rrrrumble!*" Then I squared off again.

"Look at that little china doll go!" I cried as she socked me in the forearm with her bony knuckles.

"Call me a 'doll,' huh?" she grumbled. "Ever see *Bride of Chuckie*?"

She looked so cute with her eyes all squinty and her lips curled in a snarl. I'd always thought it was funny that Raina should act so tough when she was probably the softest person around. Not just emotionally soft, like when she cried at sappy movies or fed every stray animal within a ten-mile radius of her house. But soft in a touchable way too. She was just so cuddly, like a big stuffed animal. Of course, then she'd open her mouth. . . .

"What's the matter, Lauderette?" she said, smirking. "Am I too fast for you?"

"Ooh! Bad girl Baez can talk the talk." I juked and cut sideways, reaching under her arm to pinch the inch of exposed skin between the top of her jeans and the bottom of her cropped T-shirt.

"Hey!" She whirled around to punch me, only I ducked out of the way and her fist connected with the wall behind me. "Ouch!" she exclaimed, shaking out her hand.

"Aw, man. I'm sorry, Rain. You okay?" I dropped my arms and rushed over to examine her injury.

"Ha!" she cried, poking me just above my fourth rib. It was my most vulnerable spot, and she knew it.

I stepped backward, tripped over a bucket, and fell onto my rear, accidentally pulling Raina with me.

"Oh, now you've done it. I'll show you who's boss," I cackled, rolling her over onto her back and tickling her.

"Stop it!" she hollered while laughing hysterically. "I mean it! Stop it!"

She flailed against me, but I easily pinned down her small hands with mine. "All right, Baez. You give?" I asked, my face looming only inches from hers.

Raina's smile disappeared. Her brow furrowed and her breath hit my neck in rapid bursts. "This isn't funny, Jase," she said softly. "I want to get up. Now!"

Her mood had changed so abruptly, immediately squelching out all the fun. I was confused. Just a minute earlier she'd been into it.

"I'm sorry." I scrambled off her and pulled her to her feet. "Did I hurt you?"

"No. I'm fine. I'm just . . . not in the mood."

"Sorry," I repeated, not knowing what else to say. "I was only joking around." I wasn't sure what I'd done, but I felt like a brute—a big, dopey gorilla.

An awkward silence grew between us. Without looking at me, Raina dusted off her clothes and walked to the edge of the garage. She wasn't limping, which I took to be a good sign.

"Well . . . I'd better go," she said, picking up her bulky backpack.

She tried to sound natural, but it didn't come off right. I wanted to apologize a third time, put my arms around her, and pat her head to make sure she was truly uninjured, but something made me hold back.

I jammed my hands in my pockets. "Yeah," I said casually. "I should go inside and check my messages anyway."

Raina's face twisted into a half smile. "Right. You don't want to miss Trudy in case she calls."

There was something in her voice, like a razor-sharp barb sticking off a piece of wire. Obviously she disapproved of my going after Trudy—just like she disapproved of all my other moves on girls. I considered describing how Trudy seemed better, more special than anyone else, but I was afraid Raina would be able to explain it away. And for now, I wanted to keep feeling it.

"Well, you know me," I said, making my blue eyes big and innocent-looking. "Just being a good neighbor to an out-of-town visitor."

Raina shook her head and smiled. Then she turned to go. "Right. You're a candidate for citizen of the year," she muttered as she strolled down the driveway into the darkness.

Four

T HREE DAYS LATER, Trudy still hadn't called.

I told myself she was probably busy with obligations to her aunt and uncle and cousin. After all, she'd only been in town a few days. She'd call. She had to. In the meantime, I decided to ask Darcy to come with me to the Roundup, another local hangout, on Friday night. I couldn't wait to see her legs two-stepping on the dance floor.

When Darcy and I arrived, we found Roscoe and Martian sitting at a table with Raina and a couple of her friends—Casey, our local drum major, and Renee, a drama type who got all the sexy parts in the school plays. Both girls were very cute, but Raina had made me promise never to ask them out. She said she couldn't handle getting stuck in the middle if things went sour—which things always seemed to do eventually.

Apparently her off-limits rule didn't apply to

Roscoe and Martian, though. As we approached, I could hear Roscoe talking Casey up about the time he met Drew Barrymore at the Dallas–Fort Worth Airport. He always pulls that story out when he's trying to impress a girl. And Martian just kept giggling, either because he was nervous or because he thought Roscoe was making a fool of himself.

"Hey, gang. Is it okay if we join you?" I asked once we reached their table.

"Yes!" Casey and Renee cried.

"Sure," Raina said, looking greatly relieved.

Roscoe and Martian could only stare at Darcy's legs.

I introduced everyone to Darcy and we sat down in two empty chairs. Roscoe immediately resumed his story, turning slightly so that Darcy could get the full effect.

"Anyway, she was kind of shorter than I expected her to be, but it was Drew Barrymore all right."

"Wow!" Casey exclaimed. "What did you do when you saw her?"

Roscoe lifted his shoulders casually. "I played it cool, of course. I just walked up to her and said hey, and she said hey back."

"Wow!" Casey said again, slowly shaking her head. "That's just so . . . *wow!*"

Raina caught my eye and smirked, almost making me laugh. Roscoe didn't know this, but we had heard what had really happened from his older brother, Zachary, who had been there. Apparently

Roscoe really did say "Hey," only he didn't watch where he was going and tripped over a trash can, landing facedown at Drew Barrymore's feet. That's when she yelled, "Hey!" and he ran away like a scared rabbit.

"So, Darcy," Raina began, scooting her chair closer to us. "Have you been here before?"

"Actually, this is my first time," Darcy replied. "Most of the time I hang out at Cup o' Chino's with my friends from the Academy."

"Well, what do you think of the place?" I asked.

"It's . . . okay," she said with a shrug. "Although I think using dead animals' carcasses as wall decor is extremely tasteless."

"I totally agree," Raina said, wrinkling her button nose. "The only reason I overlook it is because they've had the same mangy heads mounted on the walls for about twenty years. No fresh kill."

Darcy shifted in her chair to face Raina. "That's good. But it still demeans the poor animal. And it condones hunting just to have them up there—like advertising, almost."

"True," Raina agreed. "But hunting is a big deal around here—nothing's gonna change that. People don't think a guy's a real man if he hasn't slaughtered something by the age of eighteen. I mean, my brother . . ."

I watched nervously as Raina and Darcy leaned toward each other and began talking in hushed tones, like they were members of a secret club or something. It always bothered me when Raina got chummy with the girls I went out with. Obviously, part of me was afraid that the loyal female side of her would warn them about my so-called fear of commitment. But another part of me was worried that she might become better friends with them than she was with me. Weird, huh?

"You know, *I* hate hunting," I said loudly, trying to join the conversation. "I can't stand it." Actually, that was true. I did hate hunting. But it was more from my own bad experiences than from any philosophical opposition. The times my dad took me were awful. We had to get up painfully early and then sit around doing nothing for hours while our butts slowly turned to ice.

"I'm so glad you feel that way." Darcy smiled. "Most guys think murdering a beautiful living creature is their constitutional right. But not you." She reached over and put her hand on my arm. "You wouldn't hurt anyone."

From the corner of my eye I could see Raina give me a look, but I ignored it.

Darcy turned back around in her chair to face me and leaned in close. "Actually, I could tell when I first met you that you weren't one of those inconsiderate jerks. Normally I don't go out with someone I don't know well, but I had such a great vibe from you."

"Hey, uh, sorry to interrupt." Raina's head suddenly appeared next to Darcy's. "I didn't mean to eavesdrop, but just out of curiosity, what exactly is it about Jason that gives you that vibe?"

I shook my head at Raina's nosiness. Luckily, Darcy was such a sweet person that she didn't seem to mind.

"His eyes, for one thing. They're so expressive. And the fact that he's a musician. Artists are always so much more in touch with people's feelings. Don't you think?" she asked me.

"Oh, yeah." I nodded. "Definitely."

Raina raised a disapproving eyebrow at me.

"I knew it," Darcy went on, her eyes wide and sparkly. "Every now and then I'm really psychic about things. Like with you." She reached down and picked up my hand. "We're a perfect match. I'm trying to make the world a better place with my canvassing, just like you are with your music. It's like . . . destiny. Don't you think?"

An alarm went off inside my brain. We weren't even half an hour into the first date and the girl was already talking about destiny?

Over Darcy's shoulder I could see Raina shaking her head, flashing me a warning look. I wished she wouldn't do that. It totally ruined my concentration

"Jason?" Darcy asked. "Didn't you feel the same vibe when we met on the street?"

Raina's eyes bulged as she tried with all her facial muscles to caution me. But what did she expect me to do? Hurt the girl's feelings? It wasn't like I was promising marriage or anything.

"Oh, yeah," I said to Darcy, trying to ignore Raina as best as I could. "It was . . . just like you said."

"Uh, Jase? Could I talk to you for a sec?" Raina stood and smiled dangerously at me. "It's about the gig tomorrow."

"It can wait, Raina. We're here to have fun. Sit down and relax."

"No, I really think we should discuss this now."

"It can wait," I repeated through clenched but smiling teeth. Raina glared at me, but once again I chose to ignore it. This was my date, not hers. "Hey, this is a great song," I said to Darcy. I rose up from my chair and started to nod along to the Randy Travis tune on the jukebox. "Come on, let's dance."

"Okay," Darcy said. Raina rolled her eyes. I just gave her a smile.

I grabbed Darcy's hand and pulled her onto the huge wooden dance floor, drawing her close. Closing my eyes, I tried to concentrate on Darcy's sweet herbal fragrance and the feel of her long, strong legs pressing against mine.

"So, tell me something about yourself," Darcy murmured. "I want to know all about you."

"Like what?" I asked.

"Tell me about your music," Darcy said. "Like, what sorts of things inspire you?"

"Oh, everything really. Dogs, cats, TV shows, lunch meat—"

"People?" she asked, raising her eyebrows. "Ever write a song about a person?"

"Let's see . . . Raina and I once wrote a song about Elvis called 'Extra Side of Bacon,'" I joked.

Darcy laughed. "I mean like a love song. Ever

write one of those?" Her voice grew softer, and she seemed to step in a little closer as we danced.

Where was she going with this? "Um . . . no. Not really."

"Well, then." Darcy pulled back and gazed up at me, her face soft and expectant. "Maybe you'll be inspired to write one sometime soon."

She angled her face upward and slightly to the right, in a perfect kissing position. Somewhere in the back of my mind a voice (which sounded a little too much like Raina's) told me to hold back. But the rest of me thought, *Why not?* After all, Darcy was putting the moves on me, and I didn't want to offend her by resisting. We were just out partying on a Friday night, right? No big deal.

We stopped dancing and I cupped Darcy's face in my hands, leaning toward her. But just as our mouths were about to meet, someone tapped me on the arm.

"Excuse me. Can I cut in?" someone asked.

I looked over and saw Raina grinning at us.

This was getting ridiculous. "Not now, Raina," I said through a forced smile.

"Uh, that's okay. It's no problem," Darcy replied, glancing uncertainly from my face to Raina's. "I'd like to take a rest anyway." She turned and, with another confused look back at us, headed off the dance floor.

I stared openmouthed at Raina. It was one thing for Raina to lecture me all the time, but she had never actually meddled like this before. What had gotten into her?

"Well, don't just stand there, Jase," she said. "Be a gentleman and ask me to dance."

I grabbed her hand, yanked her toward me, and began swaying mechanically to the Dwight Yoakum tune that started up. "What do you think you're doing?" I hissed in her ear.

"What do you think *you're* doing?" she hissed back. "The girl has got it bad for you, and you're totally playing her."

"Playing her?" I repeated, laughing. "What's going on, Rain? Do you suddenly feel it's your duty to protect all women from me? Do you really think I'm so horrible?"

"You don't get it, do you?" she said, knitting her eyebrows. "I'm not so much trying to save them as I'm trying to save you!"

I scratched my head, at a total loss. "From what? A good time?"

"From *yourself.* You're a better person than this, and I hate watching you act this way."

I sighed wearily. Why was she always making things so heavy? All I wanted to do was hang out and enjoy myself, and she had to start one of her morality talks. "Come on, Rain. Lighten up," I said, jabbing her in the ribs. "It's the weekend, after all. Hey, I know. What do you say we enter Martian's name in the chicken dance contest they're having next hour?"

"No! Why is it always a joke with you?" She broke out of my grasp and stepped back, shaking her head.

"What is with you tonight?" I was completely baffled. Raina had never acted so strangely before.

Raina opened her mouth as if to say something and then shut it again. "I don't know. Look, let's just forget it," she said, her eyes softening. "But promise me you'll slow things down with Darcy. Promise me you won't say things that'll hurt her later. All right?"

"All right," I said, pulling her back toward me and resuming our dance. "You have my word. I won't do anything tonight that could hurt anyone."

I sat down in the chair, gasping for breath, and chugged a Coke as if I hadn't drunk anything in days. My lower back protested as I settled back in the seat, and I could feel muscle pulls in places I'd never realized had muscles.

"Women!" Martian exclaimed. "How did we let them talk us into that?"

"Beats me," I grumbled. "Darcy said it sounded like fun."

"Women!" Roscoe echoed.

"What are you complaining about?" Martian snapped at Roscoe. "You won second place."

We'd barely survived the chicken dance contest with our bodies and egos intact. The whole thing had been a lesson in humility, but watching Darcy do the hip shimmies had been some consolation. And at least Raina seemed to have lightened up some. She was still watching me like a hawk anytime I interacted with Darcy, though. She made certain that Darcy tagged along with her, Casey, and Renee when they went for their group bathroom visit after the contest. I wondered if she was planning on taking the opportunity to detail all my past crimes to her.

"Whoa . . . babe alert! Big babe alert!" Roscoe suddenly announced, leaning forward in his chair and pointing. "Over there, next to the jukebox. Who *is* that vision?"

Martian and I spun around, following the imaginary line from Roscoe's long, bony finger. There, scanning the music selections, stood Trudy Neidhart, looking like perfection in a sleeveless black top and tight black pants. All eyes were on her. It even seemed as though the glassy eyes of the many mounted deer heads were swiveling in her direction. But she appeared coolly oblivious.

My heart lurched, and I could feel that same magnetic pull I'd experienced when I'd first seen her. Now we'd finally get a chance to really talk! I knew it couldn't be a coincidence that she'd shown up at the Roundup. To me it seemed as if the forces of the universe were bringing us together. Of course, it also occurred to me that there weren't all that many places to hang out in Tallulah, but that thought didn't appeal to me as much.

"Who is that?" Martian gasped.

"Her name's Trudy," I said, keeping my eyes locked on her as if I were afraid she might disappear. "I met her a few days ago. She's visiting from New Orleans."

58

"Man, she's hot!" Roscoe exclaimed.

"I'd go introduce myself," Martian said, "but I'm in too much pain to get out of this chair right now."

"You just know you have no chance with her anyway," Roscoe quipped.

"Hey! I don't see *you* asking to buy her a drink," Martian countered.

"Fellas, fellas." I jumped to my feet and held up my hands. "Relax. It's just a girl. Watch. I'm going over to talk to her myself. You'll see there's nothing to fear."

"Yeah, easy for you to say," I heard Roscoe grumble as I walked away.

I approached Trudy stealthily and peered over her delicate right shoulder. "I recommend track E-twelve," I murmured, tapping my finger on the jukebox's glass case. "You just can't beat a good yodeler."

Trudy looked up at me and smiled. She didn't seem at all surprised to see me. Could she have been waiting for me? Had she known I would be there?

"Oh, really?" she said. "I was actually considering B-seventeen. Dueling banjos always does it for me."

"Well, then, you'll want G-eight."

"Or C-nineteen?"

"R-seven?"

"No, I'll take N-four."

"Bingo!" I shouted, raising a hand in the air.

Trudy laughed, lighting up the room with her picture-perfect teeth. Then she cocked her head and studied my face, narrowing her green eyes.

"You know," she said, "I was too busy to call you these past few days. I hope you aren't mad."

An immense wave of encouragement flooded through me. So she *had* been thinking about me! "Nah. Don't sweat it," I said, trying to look and sound casual. "You probably wouldn't have caught me at home anyway. I've been rather booked up myself."

"I bet you have," she said teasingly.

I smiled uncomfortably, unable to tell if she was laughing with me or at me. *With you, of course,* I silently assured myself. "So, uh . . . you here alone?" I asked.

"Who, me?" She placed her hand on her breast-bone in a dramatic gesture. "Of course not."

Damn! I thought miserably. *She's met some guy. I'm too late.* But I managed to say somewhat calmly, "Really? Who did you come with?"

Trudy chuckled. "Arlene. She's over there talking with some friends of hers."

There is a God! "Oh." I tried to mask the relief in my voice. "Well, I'm glad you came. How do you like Tallulah so far?"

She shrugged. "Fine, I guess. But tell me . . . what else is there to do here besides two-stepping and watching local pickup artists stop girls on the street?"

I swallowed and cleared my throat, trying to remain cool.

"That depends," I told her. "What sort of things do you want to do?"

"Oh, I don't know," she replied. "Something

60

new. Back home, my friends and I have gotten stuck, doing the same stuff every week."

"Like what?"

She shrugged. "Strolling the French Quarter. Going to parties. Club hopping. There's this one place, the Kit Kat Lounge, that won't let you in unless you're in a costume. At first it was a blast, but now that's gotten pretty old."

My mouth dropped open. "Wow." Then I realized I must've sounded like a country bumpkin. I cleared my throat. "Well, I'm sure there must be some great music acts to go see as well."

Trudy nodded. "Everyone I know is either in a band or follows one around."

"Cool," I said. "And you? What kind of music are you into?"

"Oh, I'm not tied to any particular type," she said, raising her eyebrows alluringly. "But I know what I like."

Geysers of sweat erupted onto my hands and underarms. "Well, then," I began, only it came out as a series of squeaks, "You should come to our gig tomorrow night at the Post."

"Maybe I will," she said. "If Arlene doesn't have anything else planned."

My mood sank. What did it take to get this girl to commit? So far every one of my invitations had been met with a "maybe" or a "we'll see."

I was starting to feel almost panicky, as if I were running out of time. The way I saw it, fate had dealt me this girl and it was up to me to find out why.

Maybe she would even inspire my music. Maybe she could help me find the soul I'd been lacking.

"Of course, I'll try my best to be there," Trudy continued. "After all, your music beats these jukebox selections any day." She met my gaze and smiled.

Volcanic activity went off inside me. *Surely she must be feeling this connection between us! How can she not?*

I leaned against the jukebox and tried to erase the silly grin I knew I had on my face. It was time to quit all the teasing and joking around. Trudy wasn't just a fun-loving groupie. This was something different—something bigger. "You know, Trudy," I began in a serious tone, "I have to say that when I first met you—"

"Excuse us," a voice came from behind me. I turned and let a couple of guys wearing LSU T-shirts look into the jukebox case. While they scanned the selections—*and* Trudy—I nervously tapped my foot and waited, impatient to continue my speech. Finally they dropped in their quarters, punched in a few numbers, and walked off. Trudy watched them go.

"Anyway," I resumed after they'd left, "I just wanted to say that—"

"Excuse me, Jason," she interrupted, giving me an apologetic look. "I really should get back to my friends now. It was really nice talking to you."

"But I—"

"I'll probably see you tomorrow night," she called out as she zigzagged around people and tables.

Skunked again! For a while things had seemed

to be cruising along nicely, then everything had fallen apart. At least she'd said she'd try to make it to the gig, though. *Probably*.

I slowly headed back to the table. Roscoe and Martian were watching me, their eyebrows raised in silent questions.

"What happened?" Roscoe asked.

"What did you talk about?" Martian added.

"Did you tell her she looked hot?"

"When are you going out with her?"

I held up my hands. "Lay off, guys. It was just some friendly small talk, that's all."

Roscoe and Martian traded shocked expressions.

"I don't believe it!" Roscoe exclaimed. "She blew you off!"

Martian shook his head in pity. "Jeez. What's the deal, dude? You losing your touch? Or have you finally met your match?"

I snorted and rolled my eyes. "Don't you guys have anything better to do than analyze my social life?"

They looked at each other again and shrugged. "No," they said together.

At that point the girls came back from the rest room, and the topic of conversation went back to our chicken dance routine. Soon everyone was laughing and joking—everyone except me.

I couldn't stop thinking about Trudy. The guys were right. I'd never had such bad luck with a girl before.

What kind of alternative dimension had I landed in?

Five

THE NEXT DAY I drove my beat-up Chevy van over to Arlene Balzen's house. On the seat beside me lay a gigantic bouquet of wildflowers: bluebonnets, black-eyed Susans, wild poppies, and some orange flowers I didn't know the name of. I also had a Natalie Merchant cassette, my acoustic guitar, a folded quilt, and a cooler full of Cokes and tuna sandwiches—just in case *someone* felt like going on a picnic. I even packed extra food in the event that Arlene had to come along.

Nothing was going to stop me from making progress with Trudy.

I couldn't believe how much effort was going into this. For me, getting girls had been ridiculously simple ever since I'd escaped junior high. I'd meet someone who seemed cute and cool, flirt a little, joke around, and eventually, when the time seemed right, ask her out. I always figured if she said no, it was no big deal. But it just so happened that no one ever turned me down.

Now I'd met someone I really liked, someone I was aching to get to know better, and I couldn't get her to say boo to me.

As I pulled into the Balzens' gravel driveway I could see Trudy sitting alone on the front porch swing, reading a magazine. I stopped the van and hopped out, holding the flowers behind my back. Trudy looked up and cast me a sly smile. Like the night before at the Roundup, she didn't seem surprised to see me.

"Hey there," I said, sauntering up to the porch. "I was driving past a field of wildflowers and thought of you. Here." I revealed the bouquet and held it out to her. "A piece of our beautiful countryside."

"Isn't that sweet?" she said in a mild tone. I couldn't tell if she was being serious or not. "I have to agree, you all have the prettiest weeds around here I've ever seen."

"They're prettier now with you holding them," I told her.

A smile freed itself, beginning at one corner of her mouth and slowly creeping across to the other. "I forgot how smooth you are," she said, shaking her index finger at me scoldingly. "Why don't you follow me inside so I can put this specimen of Tallulah countryside in some water?"

"Sure," I replied, trying not to sound too excited. We stepped through the screen door and into the Balzens' breezy foyer. The house seemed quiet and empty.

"So . . . where's Arlene and her family?"

"I don't know. Some church wingding. I pretended to be slightly ill so I could avoid it. Besides," she added, meeting my eye, "I figured someone should stay here in case a handsome, flower-bearing stranger stopped by."

Yes! I ignored the fluttering sensation in my belly and nodded coolly. "You left out 'smooth-talking.'"

"I apologize." She flashed another catlike grin. "Just wait here a minute while I go fill a vase with water. I'll try not to miss you too much."

She rounded the corner and headed into the kitchen.

You did it! I whooped inwardly, raising my fist in the air. *You're in! In her house! In the game!*

I wandered down the hallway. All I needed was a chance. I knew if only I could get her to spend some time with me, something amazing would unfold. I just couldn't ignore the signs: her incredible looks, her ultracool personality, the fact that she came from the city of music. It was as if someone had written out a prescription for the perfect girl for me. Something *had* to happen.

Just as I passed through the doorway of the dining room, a flash of color caught my eye. Three different bouquets of flowers stood atop the antique sideboard. *Maybe someone was sick. Or had a birthday,* I told myself. Still, a vague uncertainty made me walk over and investigate.

I picked up the card on the oldest and most wilted-looking of the lot. The address of a New Orleans florist was stamped on the envelope. *Trudy's hometown?* In the background I could hear her still puttering around in the kitchen. Quickly I opened the envelope. The message inside read, *Missing you. Please give me another chance. Billy.*

My heart went flat. *Who's Billy? Her boyfriend? Is he the reason she's been giving me mixed signals?*

I moved on to the next bouquet, a slightly withered collection of lilacs. Its card read, *Had fun at the rodeo. Hope to see you soon. Chase.*

Chase? Who the heck is he?

The last one, a gigantic arrangement of red roses, made my wildflowers look like . . . well, a bunch of weeds, to borrow Trudy's term. Suddenly my slick moves didn't seem so great anymore. I opened the envelope and pulled out the card. *Eleven roses for the one person beautiful enough to make an even dozen,* the message began. *Life is empty without you. Please return my calls. Rudy.*

Billy. Chase. Rudy. Which one was she with? Or, worse yet, was she with them all? A sharp pain pierced my gut, as if someone were twisting an invisible knife.

"Well, here we go. I could only find an empty mason jar, but I think it looks fine."

As Trudy's voice came closer and closer, I fumbled with the card, trying to return it to its envelope. But it slipped from my hand and fell to the floor. Trudy rounded the corner and found me on my knees with my head under the sideboard and Rudy-the-rose-guy's personal card in my hand.

"Sorry. I, uh, saw the other fl-flowers and was sort of . . . curious," I stammered, returning to my feet.

Trudy wrinkled her nose. "Oh, *those*," she said, gesturing toward my competitors' bouquets. She sighed and shook her head. "I swear, some guys just can't accept it when it's over. You know?"

Yes! So she isn't going out with any of those dudes. The clawing sensation inside me disappeared and my good mood returned. "Er, yeah. I've had that problem myself," I said, staring at her in amazement. "I mean, with girls."

Suddenly I was more optimistic than ever. She was unattached *and* completely perfect for me. Even her carefree attitude about those ex-boyfriends reminded me of myself. Those guys weren't right for her, so she had moved on. It was that simple. Just like I never hung around when the wrong girl wanted to get serious with me. Trudy and I were two free spirits who knew what we wanted in another person. And now, of course, we would find it in each other.

Trudy handed me the jar of wildflowers. Then she gathered up each of the other bouquets out of their vases and dumped them unceremoniously into a nearby wastepaper basket.

"There," she said, setting my flowers on the

sideboard among the three empty containers. "That's much better, isn't it?"

Compared to the earlier floral arrangements, my wildflowers looked puny and scraggly. Still, I liked the symbolism behind her actions.

"Speaking of our beautiful meadows," I began, taking a step toward her, "what do you say you join me for a picnic lunch? Among my many other talents, I make a mean tuna salad."

"Aw," she said, slipping her arm around mine, "I can't. I'm sorry. I'm supposed to be sick, remember? So traipsing around the great outdoors would probably blow my cover."

"Oh," I said, feeling a sharp pang of disappointment. "Will you make a speedy recovery and go out tonight? You will be coming to our gig at the Scratchin' Post, right?"

Trudy smiled and tilted her head. "Yeah, definitely. I mean, as long as we don't have other plans."

My heart dropped to my shoes. *What am I doing wrong?* The frustration was becoming unbearable.

Trudy pushed open the screen door. I hadn't even realized she'd been steering me out of the house.

"Thanks again for the flowers, Jason," she said, gently pulling me outside. "They'll remind me of you whenever I look at them—strong, wild, and cute. With maybe a hidden thorn here and there." She smiled mischievously and poked a finger into my chest.

"Uh, sure," I replied uncertainly. "Glad you like them."

I just stood there on the porch, awkwardly shifting my weight from one foot to the other. Trudy was watching me expectantly, obviously waiting for me to leave. Only I really didn't want to leave. Not without some surefire guarantee that I'd see her again soon. But I felt like a dweeb just standing there, and I didn't want to blow things by overstaying my welcome.

"Well, then," I said, stepping off the porch, "see you later, I hope."

"Yeah. See you around. Thanks for stopping by." She leaned against a wooden post and waved.

I shook my head, feeling completely powerless as I drove down the Balzens' driveway. Something weird was happening to me. I never went after anyone the way I was doing with Trudy, and I certainly wasn't used to facing resistance like this.

It must mean that Trudy's meant for me, I thought with conviction. But did Trudy feel it too? And if not, how on earth could I prove it to her?

After I left the Balzens', I drove to a nearby pasture, ate all the tuna sandwiches, and played guitar for a while. I had to do something to take my mind off Trudy, so I decided to try to write a song—one that Sylvester would think was full of soul.

Keeping Sylvester's musical tastes in mind, I attempted to write a standard blues tune. I'd never written one before, having been a staunch rock-and-roller since age two, but I knew the format. I figured that as long as I mentioned lots of depressing things and threw in some wailing guitar riffs, I'd be golden.

I cleared my head and began strumming. At first only a jumble of notes and chords came out, but then slowly, gradually, a melody emerged. That was how I'd always composed. I'd discovered that if I just trusted my guitar and listened closely, a tune always popped up. It was strange, in a way—like the music was coming through me instead of from me. But it usually worked.

Once I had the melody down, I tried to come up with some bluesy-sounding lyrics to match the mournful notes of the song. I figured I should stick with the typical heartache stuff, and after a half hour or so, I had a couple of verses worked out. It mainly repeated the line "She's run off for another man / And took my broken heart in her bag," followed by a few moans. To me, it sounded just like the blues tunes Sylvester played—almost.

Still, there was something missing. But what?

I decided to go ask Raina what she thought of the song. She'd tell it to me straight. So I loaded up my things and drove my van right to the Scratchin' Post. When I walked in, she was busily refilling saltshakers up at the front counter, seemingly in her own world.

"Hey," I said, announcing myself loudly.

She nearly dropped the enormous bag of salt. "Aaugh! Don't scare me like that!" she scolded, flicking a few stray specks of salt toward me. "If you're here for free food, you're too early. Sylvester's still cooking."

"Nah. I already ate my fill of tuna. Actually, I came to see you."

"Me? Really?" she teased, pressing her hands to her heart and batting her eyelashes. "Whatever for?"

"I just wrote a song. A good one, with soul—I think. You wanna hear it?"

"You and your quest for soul." She shook her head. "I wish you wouldn't obsess so much about this."

"Come on, Rain. It's important to me."

Raina glanced around the empty dining room and peeked into the kitchen, where Sylvester was humming and stirring something in a giant pot.

"All right. Bring your guitar and come down to the cellar with me," she said, motioning for me to follow her. "I need to get some supplies."

I smiled. "Thanks, Rain." I'd known she wouldn't let me down.

We walked through a door behind the counter and tramped down a flight of narrow, dusty steps. Even though Raina was the one doing me a favor, I knew she was more than happy to have me go downstairs with her. She *hated* that cellar. It was a spooky place, dark and musty, echoing all the squeaks and groans of the floorboards above—the

73

type of place where you'd be surprised *not* to see a couple of gauzy-looking ghosts or grotesque goblins.

The room was pretty empty except for a shelf full of restaurant supplies. It would have made a great practice space if Raina weren't so freaked out there.

"Watch your step," Raina said, flipping on the light switch as I followed her through another door at the bottom of the stairs. "Don't trip on that." She pointed to a box holding the cellar doorway open. That was another quirky thing about the place. The door tended to stick shut, since the earth underneath the building was always moving and swelling. Sylvester had once been locked in there for two hours until one of the waitpersons decided to bravely investigate the muffled cries coming up the stairwell.

Raina hugged herself and shivered. It was always surprisingly chilly down there—even in the summertime. "I'm going to check around for a box of napkins," she told me. "You go ahead and serenade me with this new song of yours."

I dug in my back pocket for my pick and checked my tuning. Then I launched into the first few sad chords. As I played, Raina stopped rummaging around the storage shelf to watch me closely. Her eyes softened, and she looked thoughtful—emotional, even. My heart lifted. I figured I must have hit pay dirt with the song.

When I was done, I paused dramatically for a

few seconds, letting the final note reverberate through the stale air. "Well, what do you think?" I asked, ready for her to lay on the praise.

She nodded, wiping stray blond wisps of hair away from her eyes. "Um . . . it's good, Jase. Nice guitar work. And that raspiness in your voice was a nice touch. But . . ." She paused, biting her lip. "Well, you might want to redo the chorus somewhat. The phrase 'Since she left me for a guy named Joe, my heart's aching like a big stubbed toe' sounds a little too . . . Billy Ray Cyrus."

My heart did a tumble dive to the floor. "You don't like it."

Raina shook her head. "No. No, it's fine. I mean, you're trying out some new sounds, and that's always cool. And I can come by sometime and help you smooth it out—if you want."

"Forget it," I muttered.

Raina sighed and sat down on a nearby crate. "Look. Maybe you can't write about having a broken heart when you've never really experienced it. Face it, Jase. You get every girl you want."

"Not every girl," I mumbled, taking off my guitar and leaning it against a shelf.

"I see," Raina said, her mouth curving into a smile. "I thought something was up when you showed up here so early. I figured you'd be hanging out with Darcy right about now."

"Not Darcy. I had . . . other plans, but things didn't go the way I expected." I plopped down on the box opposite from Raina and exhaled heavily.

"I need your advice on something, but promise me you won't give me a hard time about it, okay?"

Raina's forehead bunched up into an expression of concern. "Okay. I promise," she said. Then she reached out and tapped my knee with her long, tapered fingers. "What's up, Jase? You look really out of it."

"It's Trudy. I've been trying to get her to go out with me, but nothing seems to work." I told her about my conversation with Trudy at the Roundup the night before, and about her hot/cold signals that morning at the Balzens'.

"I just can't get anywhere with her, Rain. The potential is there, I know it is. But I always come up empty, and I don't know why." I glanced down to the floor, making little circles on the dusty floor with the toe of my sneaker. Then I looked back at Raina.

She cocked her head and frowned. "She sounds like a total snob. Are you sure she's even worth the trouble?"

"Oh, yeah, no doubt. She's like no one I've ever met before. Classy, cool, totally sophisticated. I can't let this opportunity go by."

"I swear, Jase," Raina muttered, shaking her head, "sometimes I don't know whether to laugh at you or slap you around. Darcy's a really sweet girl. Why do you want to go after someone else when you know she's so into you?"

I shrugged. "Trudy's special. Doesn't that mean anything?"

Raina's face stiffened. "Depends on how you define 'special.'"

"Come on. Don't be mad at me." I leaped off the box and kneeled next to her. "I really need your help with this, Rain. Can't you stop being a girl for a minute and just be my friend?"

A strange expression darkened her features. "This really means a lot to you, doesn't it?" she asked, examining me with her cocoa-colored eyes.

"Yes! I've never felt this way before. Ever." I inched my face even closer to hers and scrunched up my forehead like a sad golden retriever. "Please, Rainbow?" I begged. "I just need you to tell me what I'm doing wrong. Please?"

"All right! All right! Just stop with the eager-puppy routine before you have an accident."

I smiled. I'd been sure she would come around.

Raina stood up and paced the room, tapping an index finger against her chin. "Okay. You say she saw you pick up Darcy, right?"

I nodded. "Right."

"And she must've seen you with Darcy at the Roundup."

"Uh, maybe."

"Well, it seems to me that this girl doesn't like sharing things. And if she thinks you're already dating Darcy"—she turned and looked at me—"she's not going to want to be a second-stringer. Get it?"

My mouth fell open. Why hadn't I thought of that? "Hey, yeah. That makes sense."

"Is Darcy coming to the gig tonight?"

"Yeah. She said she'd be here."

"And you also asked Trudy?"

"Aw, man!" I exclaimed, whacking my hand against my forehead. "I did it again, didn't I? That's it. I've gotta break things off with Darcy and show Trudy I'm all hers."

Raina sighed. "You sure that's what you want to do?"

"I'm sure. It's no big deal, really. I mean, Darcy and I were just having fun. It's not like we had something serious, right?"

"With you? No. Definitely not."

"Yes! You saved me!" I hollered, reaching over and giving Raina a big bear hug. "Thanks, Rain. I don't know why I didn't even think of that."

"Just promise me one thing," Raina said, smoothing her apron after my frenzied embrace.

"Sure. Anything."

Raina stared into my eyes. "Promise me you'll go easy on Darcy."

"Who, me?" I asked, flashing my dimples angelically. "I'm the picture of easy."

Six

"**Y**OU KNOW WHAT, Jason? You're a total jerk!" Darcy's hands were clenched into fists, and her eyes had turned watery.

A hush came over the crowd of people already congregating on the deck to watch our gig. I hadn't wanted to do this in public, but I needed to call things off with Darcy in case Trudy showed up that night. I wasn't going to let anything spoil my chances this time. But I did hate to see a sweet girl like Darcy cry.

"I mean, you're, you're . . . an inconsiderate slimeball!" Darcy continued, the tears flowing freely down her cheeks now.

For someone who professed to be psychic, Darcy sure hadn't seen this coming. I, on the other hand, was overcome by a definite feeling of déjà vu. And it wasn't pleasant.

"Look, Darcy," I said softly, hoping she would

follow suit and lower her voice as well—or at least stop crying. "I'm sorry, but I just—"

"Don't give me your lame apologies!" she said through clenched teeth. "I never want to see you again! Ever!"

Before I could say anything more, Darcy pushed past me and ran off. I watched her long legs propel her across the deck, through the restaurant, and out the main door. Only then did I breathe a sigh of relief.

"Jason? Are you all right?" Kimmy suddenly appeared beside me.

"What's *her* problem?" Junie McAllister asked, walking up behind Kimmy.

Brenda ran over from the bar. "What is with her?" she said. "Are all the girls who go to the Academy, like, totally nuts?"

"It's no big deal," I said, trying to laugh off my embarrassment. "Some people just lose it over little things. You know?"

"I'm not like that," Kimmy said, smiling.

"Neither am I," Brenda echoed.

"So." Junie took a step closer to me. "I guess you won't be seeing *her* again, huh?"

"Uh . . . no," I replied. "At least I hope not. I have a feeling that if I ran into her again, she'd be pointing a weapon at me."

The girls erupted into a chorus of giggles, and the humiliation I felt over Darcy's little scene subsided somewhat.

"Jason!" Raina called from the stage. "Come over here. It's almost show time."

"Excuse me," I said, smiling apologetically. "My mom's calling."

They laughed once again as I made my way across the room. Raina stood waiting for me, a fleck of irritation in her eyes. "What happened, Jase? I thought you said you were going to take it easy on her."

"*Me* take it easy on *her*? She's the one who went off the deep end," I protested. "They could probably hear her yelling in the next parish."

"Oh, stop complaining. You did what you wanted. Now you've got Darcy off your back so you can save yourself for Trudy the Snooty."

"That's true," I said, smiling to myself.

Raina pursed her lips and regarded me a moment. "Don't you feel the teensiest bit sorry for Darcy? Do any cells in your body feel guilty at all?"

I sighed and plopped down on the edge of the stage. Raina perched next to me, still studying my expression. I swear, the girl can read me like a manual. It's never any use trying to bend the truth with her.

"Of course I feel bad," I replied. "I just don't understand why girls freak out so much when I call it quits. I mean, it's not like I'm calling off a serious relationship or anything."

"It's because you're the type of guy girls would *like* to get serious with," Raina explained. Then she twisted up her mouth in a sneer and butted her shoulder against mine. "Although *why* they would want to is a mystery to me."

"Hey!" I said, tugging on her French braid. "You should be happy for me. After all, I'm finally thinking seriously about a girl."

"I am," she said, smiling weakly. "Really. I just hope Trudy is everything you think she is."

Her concern both touched and amused me. Raina was worried? For years she'd been on my case about my treatment of girls. Now I was actually focusing on one incredible girl for a change, and she was all uneasy.

Raina had always been easier to figure out than most girls, but I guessed that even she had her schizophrenic moments.

"Come on," she said, standing up. "Let's find Roscoe and Martian and get this show on the road."

"Already?" I asked, glancing at my watch.

Sure enough, it was eight o'clock. I did a quick scan around the room for Trudy, but I didn't see her or Arlene anywhere. Disappointment squeezed my insides.

"Aw, Jase. Don't tell me you're worried your dream girl won't show," Raina said, reading my thoughts once again.

"Yeah, right. I'm never worried," I replied, grinning casually.

But for the first time in years, I really was.

Ten o'clock and she's still not here! I grumbled inwardly. It was close to the end of our set, and Trudy still hadn't shown up. I felt strangely bitter, as if I'd been stood up. She'd said she was coming. I tried to tell myself it was no big deal, that her relatives must have made other plans, like she'd said might happen, but it didn't make me feel any better.

I leaned over my guitar and tried to vent my frustration during my solo, scrunching up my face as I plucked and stretched the notes. A couple of girls in the audience squealed. That made me feel a little better. At least the gig was going great—*really* great, in fact.

Behind me, Martian was drumming out a perfect rhythm, and to my left, Roscoe was in his own little bass world. His eyes were shut and his head bobbed along to the beat. Raina was in the zone too, swaying back and forth as she pounded on her keyboard.

Yep, everyone was totally on that night . . . except maybe me. *Get with it, Jason,* I ordered myself. I resolved to forget about Trudy and to concentrate on the music instead.

"*And she says baby,*" I sang into the microphone, trying to tap into the energy onstage.

Out in the crowd I could see Brenda doing her little dance. She caught my eye and smiled. I smiled back. *Just cut loose,* I told myself. This *is what it's all about.*

Sure enough, the more I put into the show, the better I felt. I shut my eyes and belted out the lyrics with as much emotion as I could muster. I danced around, tapped my foot, and even added some fancy guitar work. The audience seemed to feel it too. And hearing them whoop and whistle only made me play harder. By the end of the song I was completely energized.

"Man! You were really cranking it out on that one!" Roscoe hollered over the applause.

"Yeah, it was cool!" I replied with a smile. "I actually busted my pick!" I held it up so Roscoe could see the missing point on the triangle.

"Whoa," he murmured. "You've got the power tonight!"

I grinned and absently tossed the pick offstage. A couple of girls shrieked and grabbed for it. Roscoe cracked up. "Look at that! What would they do if you took off your shirt?"

I laughed and shook my head. Roscoe was right—I did have the power that night. Everything would have been perfect if only Trudy could have been there to see me in all my glory.

Raina tapped my arm as I reached onto a nearby amp for a new pick. "Jase," she said, frowning, "this ego trip of yours is fine as long as you limit it to making kissy faces and wiggling your butt. But please don't get carried away and start stripping—or tossing your guitar to some squealing sophomore."

My mouth dropped open. "What? I'm not doing anything except playing some killer guitar riffs."

She rolled her eyes. "Save it for the Grammys, Mr. Rock Star."

I ignored her and turned back around, plucking

out a few chords to test my new pick. *Raina's just being a killjoy*, I thought. *All I'm doing is giving everyone a great show. Besides, it's the only thing that's helping me keep my mind off—*

Suddenly my heartbeat sped up to a faster tempo. In the back of the room, perched regally on a barstool, was Trudy. She had come after all!

She sat like a Michelangelo statue, hands on her knees, head slightly tilted, a look of composure on her face. Even her skin had the cool smoothness of marble, especially around the curves of her neck and shoulders. Only her jet-black hair and the wispy slip of her aqua dress kept her from looking as though she'd been pried out of a fountain.

I knew just what to do. Quickly I spun around and whispered instructions to the rest of the band, then turned back to the microphone.

"I'd like to dedicate this next song to the gorgeous girl sitting at the bar," I announced.

Trudy looked right at me, her mouth curling into her trademark grin.

A murmur went up from the crowd. Everyone's heads snapped back and forth from Trudy to me.

"Who's that?" I heard someone whisper.

"He's never dedicated a song to anyone before!" someone else exclaimed.

On my cue, the band started up a rollicking version of "Devil with a Blue Dress." As I sang, I kept my eyes locked on Trudy, studying her reaction. She totally dug it. Or at least it seemed that way. Instead of blushing or acting all coy, the way I

85

expected her to, she just smiled and met my gaze head-on, watching me as I watched her. I swear, that girl knew just how to get me.

When the song ended, Trudy clapped, then began digging in her purse. I couldn't see what she was doing, but I figured she needed to pay for her drink or something. I hoped that didn't mean she was on her way out.

"That was a slick move, Lauderette," Roscoe said, nudging me. "Only you sort of ruined the evening for a lot of other people. Did you see the death stares coming from the crowd?" He shook his head and cackled loudly. "I sure hope it worked, because if you strike out with that girl again, you won't have any backups."

His laughter died out as Trudy suddenly appeared at the edge of the stage.

"Nice show," she said with a wry grin.

"Thanks," I responded. After waiting all evening, I couldn't believe she was actually there, in person, talking to me. Now I could finally make my move. "So," I added, stepping off the stage, "can I get you another drink?"

"Sorry," she said. "I've got to go home."

"You're leaving?" My heart shuddered as all hopes for the evening came crashing down.

"Here. I wanted to give you this first." She pressed a small piece of paper into my hand and closed my fingers around it. "See you later." Then before I could say anything more, she turned and headed out of the restaurant.

I just stood there watching her, too stunned to move.

"Oh, dude! That's harsh!" Roscoe exclaimed.

"Man!" Martian said. "She turned you down flat. *Again!*"

"Shut up, guys!" Raina ordered. She walked up beside me and gave me a gentle nudge. "Hey. You okay?"

I was too numb with frustration to respond. Instead I looked down and slowly unfolded the piece of paper in my hand.

"Jason? You all right?" Raina repeated.

After a brief pause I glanced up and stared straight into her eyes. "I'm great, Rain," I replied, new confidence flooding through me. "In fact, I've never been better."

I held up the scrap of paper. On it, in big, loopy script, Trudy had written: *Pick me up tomorrow evening at seven.*

Seven

I STOOD IN the Balzens' flower-filled dining room, pacing and humming. On the sideboard by the doorway sat two new flower arrangements—a collection of yellow carnations and another bunch of roses, this time pink. My wildflowers had already faded, drooped over the edge of the mason jar as if they were bowing down to their obvious superiors. I made a mental note to buy an incredibly showy bouquet sometime soon.

In the meantime, I wondered who the new flowers were from. I slowly bent over to read the cards, pretending to be checking my reflection in the sideboard's small oval mirror.

"Don't worry. You look great." Arlene's voice came from behind me.

Arlene had met me at the door earlier and had announced that Trudy was still getting ready. For fifteen straight minutes she sat at the dining room table, chomping on an apple and making small talk with me. It was nice of her, but soon enough we ran out of things to say on such safe topics as school, mutual friends, and my gigs at the Scratchin' Post, and I started wondering what could be holding up Trudy.

Since it was impossible to read the cards without Arlene's noticing, I decided to squeeze some information out of her.

I casually tucked my fingers into my front jeans pockets and strolled around the dining room table. "So, Arlene," I began offhandedly, "I bet you and your cousin have been having a blast together. Is it like a slumber party every night?"

She shook her head and giggled. "Actually, I don't see her much. She mostly does her own thing. Since she brought her own car and all, she doesn't need me to haul her around."

"I saw you two at the Roundup the other night. And you brought her to a couple of my gigs. That was cool of you."

"Yeah, well, 'brought her' is about the extent of it," she said with a shrug. "After we get someplace, she always takes off on her own, scoping out any and every good-looking guy—especially college guys. You know, it's weird. She's the same age as us, but she says high-school guys are too young for me."

I let this bit of news settle in gradually. Trudy mainly liked older guys? That would explain why she seemed so much more sophisticated than every other girl. Of course, that also meant I had no chance of impressing her. Suddenly my nerves felt as tight as guitar strings.

Arlene cocked her head and looked at me. "But Trudy did make an exception in your case," she remarked matter-of-factly. "She must really like you."

I smiled, feeling a little better. *Must really like me?* I held on to Arlene's last comment like a life preserver.

"Okay, let's go." Trudy suddenly breezed into the room, looking amazing in some white capri pants and a blue top that was tied in a knot at her midriff.

Seeing her made me feel a *lot* better.

"Hey!" I said a little too loudly. "You look great."

"Thanks. That's why you had to wait so long. I absolutely love these pants, but they got all wrinkled in the suitcase. I've spent the last five minutes ironing in my underwear," she said, laughing.

I chuckled awkwardly, overcome by the mental vision of Trudy half dressed and surrounded by steam.

"That doesn't explain the other fifteen minutes you kept him waiting," Arlene called from the table.

Trudy rolled her eyes. "Yes, we're all very impressed with how well you can tell time, Arlene," she shot back. Then she glanced at her watch and frowned. "She's right, though. I hope I didn't make us late for whatever you had planned."

Actually, she had. I'd been hoping to take her to the new sci-fi/horror flick, thinking that slime-covered aliens popping onto the screen with no warning might make her jump in my lap a few times. Either that, or I figured the sappy romance movie might put her in a cuddly mood. Unfortunately, both movies had already started.

"Don't worry about it," I said, shrugging. "There are a couple of movies at the Cineplex that don't start for a while. I'm sure we'll find something there we like."

"I'm sure we will," she repeated, smiling slyly.

As we walked toward the front door Arlene called to us, "You guys have a good time!"

Trudy walked outside without responding.

"Thanks, Arlene," I called back. "See you soon."

"Yeah. Good luck, Jason," I heard her mutter as the door swung shut.

I stopped in midstep. Why did she think I would need it?

Trudy decided on a Matt Damon movie. I had to hold myself back from groaning. In the past month I'd seen that film three different times on three separate dates.

Still, I forced myself to say, "Sounds great," and got in the long ticket line. After all, I was just psyched to finally have an evening with her—no matter what we ended up seeing.

The line was moving at the pace of an arthritic snail, but it gave us a chance to talk. I asked her about the New Orleans music scene. She described the clubs where she and her friends hung out, and all the local groups that were landing contracts with record companies. I couldn't believe how hip she was about everything.

"You know what's huge right now?" she asked. "Lounge acts. All the bands are hiring saxophone players, wearing shiny suits, and poufing up their hair. Hey! Maybe you guys could try that."

A minor flash of panic seared through me. She thought we needed a gimmick. "I don't think so," I replied, laughing nervously. "No way could I get any of those guys in suits. Besides, no one in Tallulah swing-dances."

"But you're not planning on staying in Tallulah forever, are you?" she asked, tilting her head. "You seem like someone who has his sights on bigger things. With the right look, you guys could go far. I'm sure of it."

My smile widened. Although I wasn't quite sure what she meant by the "right look," I liked her enthusiasm. Local girls were always telling me how much they liked my songs and how cool they thought the band was, but Trudy's opinion mattered more. For one thing, she seemed to know a lot more about the music scene. Plus, the fact that she wasn't one of our groupies made her compliment feel more real. As though we'd actually earned it.

"I do hope someday we'll play to stadium crowds," I admitted. "And we talk sometimes about moving out to the West Coast after graduation and trying to hook up with an agent."

"You should! That's what all the bands do."

I beamed back at her. This girl was, without a doubt, the coolest girl I'd ever met. "Of course," I said, standing on my toes to peer over the heads of people in front of us, "first I need to get out of this ticket line. I can't believe it's taking so long."

She shook her head. "It *is* moving slowly. I'll go take a look inside." Trudy strolled over to the glass doors and peeked into the lobby. Watching her, I had the sudden, bizarre thought that I would be happy to look at Trudy every day for the rest of my life. She was that beautiful.

Eventually Trudy turned and trotted back over with a huge smile on her face. As she came closer she lifted her hand out toward me. My heart skipped. Returning her smile, I placed my left hand on her outstretched palm and pulled her up beside me.

"No, no," she said, laughing, patting my left hand with her right. "I was going to ask you for some money. I thought I could go inside and buy us popcorn and sodas while you stay in line for the tickets."

"Oh . . . sure," I replied, feeling a bit deflated—and stupid. "Great idea."

Trudy let go of my hand so I could open up my wallet and pull out a twenty.

"Here," I said, handing her the bill. "You know,

they have this popcorn size called the Sweethearts' Sack. What do you think? Are we ready to take such a step?"

"Ooh. Sounds exciting," she murmured, tapping her finger on the tip of my nose and sending tingles throughout my body. Then she turned and headed through the double glass doors of the lobby.

I sighed and shuffled my shoes on the concrete. The air around me suddenly seemed cold without her near. *Man, what's with this line? By the time we get tickets Matt Damon will have false teeth!*

"Well, well," came a familiar voice from behind me. "Don't tell me Jason is at the movies by himself tonight." Shelly Armstrong appeared by my side, a wry smile twisting her heavily glossed lips.

Just what I needed to help pass the time: a bitter ex-girlfriend.

"Hey, Shel," I said. "No, I'm with someone. She's inside getting us some drinks."

"Really?" She raised an eyebrow. "So who is it? Which lucky girl are you playing games with this week?"

"No one," I said with a frustrated sigh. "But I *am* taking someone to a movie. You wouldn't know her. She's not from around here."

"Well, that explains it. She'd have to be from Botswana not to know your reputation."

I tapped my foot impatiently. *Why can't she just leave me alone?* "And what about you, Shelly? Who's your guy for tonight? Matt Damon?"

She narrowed her eyes at me, and I could tell I touched a nerve. "No. I'm here with friends—*real* friends. Isn't that what you offered to be? What was that closing line of yours again? 'Sorry, Shel. It's been fun, but why don't we just be friends or something?'"

By now other people in line had turned around to watch us, some of them already stuffing their faces with popcorn—as if we were the show they'd come to see.

I shook my head in disbelief. Why did she seem to think I owed her something? "So what? What's so wrong about offering friendship?"

"Nothing, if you really mean it. But you were just saying it to soften the blow." Shelly shook her head. "It's not that you broke up with me that makes you a slimeball, it's the *way* you broke it off. You showed no respect for my feelings whatsoever." Her voice softened a little, and she looked into my eyes with an expression vaguely resembling pity. "You've got no heart, Jason. No soul."

Jeez, I thought. *Now she sounds like Sylvester. At least Trudy isn't here to see all this. Where is she anyway?* Craning my neck, I peered around Shelly's head to look into the lobby. Trudy was deep in conversation with the snack bar guy, a big football-player type. I would have felt uneasy except that the pink-and-white paper hat he had to wear made him look really dorky.

"You know, I'm not the only one who feels this way," Shelly continued in her ridiculous rant. "I could start a club of all the girls you've led on and then tossed aside."

"So why don't you?" I asked flatly.

Shelly shook her head, again looking almost sorry for me. "You know, one of these days you're going to get a taste of your own medicine."

"Whatever you say, Shel," I muttered, staring up at the dimming sky.

"Here we go," Trudy announced, carefully balancing a cardboard tray of snacks as she walked toward us. "I got us a deal on the popcorn. Oh, and I wasn't sure what you liked to drink, so I got you a Dr Pepper." She paused as she caught sight of Shelly. A wary smile crept onto her face. "Uh . . . hello there. Should I have gotten three drinks?"

"No," I said. "Trudy, this is Shelly. She was just leaving."

Shelly ignored me and stood her ground, looking Trudy over. "Watch out for this guy," she finally said, wagging her thumb at me. "He's a total player." Then she spun around on the heels of her sandals and marched to the back of the line.

Wonderful. I hoped Trudy didn't take Shelly's statement to heart.

But right when I was about to apologize for her behavior, Trudy burst out laughing.

"Charming girl!" she exclaimed sarcastically.

I smiled. "Isn't she? I don't know why I ever broke up with her."

"You know, I find that harassing my old boyfriends *always* makes them want to take me back. You mean it doesn't work with you?" she asked, opening her mouth in pretend shock.

"Nope. I guess I'm just weird that way," I joked, shrugging. "For some strange reason, I'd much rather spend time with you."

Trudy grinned playfully, her green eyes lighting up with amusement. "Well, it's going to take a lot more than a few ex-girlfriends to scare me off tonight. You *player,* you!"

We were still chuckling when we bought our tickets and sat down in the theater. Once again I felt full of hope. I'd never laughed with a girl like that. Well, except for Raina, of course, but she didn't count.

I'd never stopped to think what my dream girl would be like, but Trudy was so clearly her. She was just so . . . cool. And she had to feel the perfect vibes between us now.

Yes, the evening was definitely shaping up to be a good one.

I pulled the van down the Balzens' driveway and cut the engine. We'd had a blast at the movie theater, and now all I wanted to do was show Trudy how I felt with a meaningful good-night kiss. I unbuckled my seat belt and turned to face her in the darkness.

"I had a great time," I said, leaning my left arm against the dash. "Well . . . most of it was great. I'm sorry about Shelly."

"Oh, please." Trudy waved off my comment

with her hand. "Don't worry. I know the type."

"So when can we see each other again? Wanna meet for lunch tomorrow?"

She shook her head. "I have plans. Sorry."

"Okay. How about the next day, then?" I asked, leaning toward her.

"You really don't waste time, do you?" she said, shoving my shoulder playfully. "Is this how you usually operate?"

I pulled back, startled by her comment. "Uh . . . no," I said, drooping my head slightly. "I mean, I just wanted to spend time with you, that's all." The whiny quality of my voice made me wince.

"We have plenty of time, Jason," she said with a chuckle. "Don't rush things. Let's just have fun for now."

I sighed and plopped back against my seat. "Funny," I mumbled. "Raina's been telling me that I move too fast. But I guess I didn't want to listen to her."

Trudy's eyebrows shot up. "Oh? Who's Raina?"

"My best friend. You've seen her. She plays keyboards in our band."

"Ah, yes. The cute blonde." She squinted at me and frowned. "You sure she's *just* a friend?"

"Positive. Although sometimes she's more of a pain than a buddy," I grumbled. "She's always trying to run my social life."

"Sounds like an interesting relationship." Trudy's voice went flat, snapping me back to the present.

"Oh, sorry. I don't know why I'm talking about

her right now," I said, leaning forward again. "I'd much rather talk about you. So when *can* I see you again?"

Trudy undid her seat belt and yawned, stretching her arms up high.

"How about this weekend?" she asked, settling back in her seat.

That seemed much too long to wait, but I didn't want to scare her off. "Sounds great," I lied. "You know, there's a big party going on after our gig Saturday."

"A party?" she asked, her eyes widening.

"Yeah. Tony Brewer's parents always go up north somewhere for a couple of weeks in the summer, and his older brother gets a couple of kegs. It's, like, the social event of the season. You feel like going?"

"Count me in," Trudy replied, smiling broadly.

She looked so gorgeous. The lights from the front porch beamed onto the graceful curve of her neck, making it look like the stem of a crystal wineglass. And as I stared, the glare of headlights passing on the road behind us flickered in her green eyes. I was mesmerized.

In order for two people to kiss in the front seats of a van, each person has to lean in toward the other, so they can meet in the gap between the seats. Trudy wasn't budging.

I rose from my seat and headed toward her, my arms outstretched.

"You are so beautiful," I murmured, aiming my

lips in a perfect trajectory toward hers.

Suddenly, in a quick, catlike motion, Trudy retracted her head, opened the door, and slipped out of the car.

"See you Saturday," she said with a crooked smile, then strode off toward the house.

Eight

"TRUDY, TRUDY," I sang. "You're my . . ."

Let's see . . . what rhymes with Trudy? *Tutti-frutti? Hot-patootie? Shake your booty?* I sighed. Why couldn't she have an easy name, like Anne or Jean?

I was sitting cross-legged on my bed, playing my acoustic and trying once again to write a song filled with soul. I figured if anyone could inspire me, it would be Trudy. Since our date two days earlier, I'd been thinking of no one else. I was either crazy about her or just plain crazy.

Even my music seemed to be suffering. I'd canceled our band practice Sunday evening so I could take Trudy to the movies, and I hadn't rescheduled it yet. (I wanted to keep my nights free in case she called.) And now I couldn't even get down a few lines on a new song. That had never happened before. Never.

I strummed a C chord and started over. "Hey, Trude . . . I'm your dude . . ." *Forget it! This isn't happening!*

Sylvester always told me to plug my emotions into my music, and I'd hoped all the frustration I felt over Trudy might help me come up with a really moving song. Unfortunately, everything I had cranked out so far was about as soulful as a nursery rhyme.

I started over, changing the key with a higher, sadder E chord.

"Trudy, Trudy . . . you . . ."

Rrrring!

The high-pitched chirp of my cordless phone suddenly blended into the melody. I set down my guitar and picked up the receiver, praying that my music had worked some black magic and had caused Trudy to call me.

"Hello?" I answered, trying hard not to sound as hopeful as I felt.

"Good afternoon," came a woman's voice on the other end. "This is Robyn Foster, booking manager for Tallulah Fourthfest. May I please speak with Jason Loder . . . Later . . ."

My stomach did a somersault. "Lauderette? Jason Lauderette? This is him. I mean, he. This is he."

"Yes, Mr. Lauderette. I'm calling to let you know that we received your demo last week, and after careful review, our judging committee has decided to offer the Bankheads a spot in this year's Fourthfest."

"You . . . ? I . . . ? We . . . ?" It was hard to breathe. Short bursts of air escaped from my mouth, weakening my words. "That's amazing!" I finally blurted out.

We'd done it! We'd actually made Fourthfest! The realization was almost too much for my brain to handle on its own. I couldn't wait to tell Raina. She'd freak!

"We'd like you to play the two P.M. slot," Ms. Foster continued. "That's right after Paul Minor and His Orchestra, and right before Johnny Law. Will that work with your band's schedule?"

"Sure! I mean, luckily we happen to have that time open."

"Good. We'll be sending you a contract and other legal papers in the mail. If you have any questions, don't hesitate to call me. My card will be attached."

"Sounds great. Thank you, Ms. Foster. Ma'am. Thanks a lot."

Long after the line disconnected, I remained sitting on my bed, cradling the receiver against my face. A warm, tingly sensation spread over me, as if I were slowly being microwaved. *We were in! We did it!*

Snapping out of my trance, I reactivated the phone and punched the number one speed dial. As soon as I heard Raina's voice, I began shouting out instructions.

"Raina! Assemble the gang! We're having an emergency rehearsal. Now!"

"Jase? Is that you? Are you okay?" she asked, sounding slightly alarmed.

"I mean it. If you guys are not here in the next fifteen minutes, I'll . . . I'll play the tapes of our 1997 practice jams on the local radio stations."

"Jeez. You *are* cracking up. All right, chief. Whatever you say."

I hung up the phone and flew down the stairs, broadcasting my news to my parents.

"Mom! Dad! We're in! We made Fourthfest!"

By the time I reached the living room, Mom was running in from the back bedroom, a leaky watering can in her hand, and Dad was hightailing it from the kitchen.

"What? What's wrong?" Dad asked.

"I said, we made Fourthfest." I ran over to Mom and waltzed her around the room. Water sloshed over the sides of the can and dribbled onto the carpet. "I just talked with the booking manager on the phone. The Bankheads have a two o'clock slot."

"Oh, honey!" Mom gasped. "That's so . . . cool!"

"Fourthfest? What's Fourthfest?" Dad asked.

"You know. It's that local music festival," I replied impatiently. "It's a big deal."

"I see," he said, still looking confused. "How much do you get paid?"

"Nothing, Dad. It's a showcase for local talent. You play for a huge crowd and get lots of free publicity. And sometimes record agents show up too."

"It's a big deal, Jim," Mom said, echoing my words.

"Well, that's great, son," Dad said, clapping me awkwardly on the back. "Congratulations."

"Have you told your friends yet?" Mom asked. "Does Raina know?"

I shook my head. "Not yet. I want it to be a surprise. Everyone's on their way over for an emergency rehearsal."

"Rehearsal?" Dad grumbled. Mom stopped him with a warning look. "Well, okay. But try to keep it down, okay?"

I rolled my eyes. "Okay, Dad."

As much as they tried, I knew Mom and Dad just didn't understand how important making Fourthfest was to me. But I wasn't going to let that get me down. We'd gotten the break, and that was all that mattered. After all, it wasn't every day that your ultimate dream came true.

"Whoo-hoo!"

"We did it, man!"

"Da Bankheads gonna be da bomb!"

Raina, Martian, and Roscoe hopped around in their own little victory dance, shouting and high-fiving each other. After the mixed reaction from my parents, it was great to see them whooping it up.

"Man! We're big-time!" Roscoe shouted. "I mean, how many people usually show up for this shindig?"

"I think last year's count was around five thousand," Raina said.

"Whoa," Martian said, looking a little dazed. "I

think I need to sit down." He stumbled over to an old steamer trunk in the corner of the garage and plunked himself down on it.

"And there's talk that some major label A&R guys will be there," I added, bouncing up and down like a preschooler. "And MTV might cover it too!"

"We're gonna be famous!" Roscoe cheered.

"You know, Jase," Raina said, her voice suddenly serious, "we really owe all this to you. You made this a goal of ours and pushed us toward it. We would've been perfectly happy to just play Saturday-night gigs at the Scratchin' Post and never aim any higher."

Roscoe clapped me on the back, nearly toppling me over. "The dude knows how to dream big!"

"Five thousand people," Martian muttered from his corner. "Whoa."

"Come on, guys. We did this together." I slung my arm around Raina and slugged Roscoe's upper arm.

"But you led the way," Raina went on. She twisted around and stared up at me, her eyes wide and insistent. "Face it. This is really *your* dream, Jase. We just hopped on for the ride."

I opened my mouth to protest again, but Raina stopped me, reaching up and squishing my cheeks together with her hands.

"Stop acting all humble!" she shouted. Then she let go of my face and leaned forward, lowering her voice to a whisper. "It's finally happening, Jase," she said, smiling. "You *did* it. Be proud!"

I looked down at her and stretched my sore cheeks into a grin. Leave it to Raina to say what I needed to hear. Somehow I'd known she'd be the one to fully understand what it all meant.

A high volume of moisture suddenly filled my eyes, and I quickly turned around to focus on a microphone before anyone noticed. "Okay. Enough celebration," I called out. "We've got two weeks to become Fourthfest's answer to the Beatles, so let's get to work."

Martian jumped up and trotted over to his drum set, shaking his head. "Two weeks! Whoa."

"'Bout time we jam," Raina said, walking over to her keyboard. "I was beginning to think you didn't love us anymore."

"Yeah. I figured you'd ditched us to run off with that Trudy girl," Roscoe added, wiggling his eyebrows. "How are things going with the new conquest anyway?"

"Fine," I replied stiffly. "Not that it's any of your business." The mere mention of Trudy's name brought my frustration welling back up to the surface, dousing my good mood.

"You going to see her again soon?" Martian asked. "Or have you already broken up with her?"

I exhaled heavily. Normally I'd have tolerated the guys' teasing with mild amusement, but hearing them use their lame jokes on Trudy wasn't at all funny.

"I'm seeing her Saturday," I said. "She's coming

to the gig, and then we're going to Tony Brewer's bash together."

"Have you told her about Fourthfest? That she's going out with a soon-to-be major rock star?" Roscoe asked.

"No," I said, pausing in the middle of a strum. "I didn't." Why *hadn't* I told her yet? "But I can't wait to," I continued, smiling to myself. "She'll freak." Then I had a sudden thought. "Darn! I should've asked that management lady about getting a backstage pass for her."

"Wait. You're planning on taking her to Fourthfest?" Raina asked. The note of shock in her voice surprised me.

"Yeah," I answered. "So?"

"But that's two weeks from now," Roscoe commented. I could hear an anguished "whoa" from behind Martian's drum set.

"So?" I asked again.

"Dude, you never keep a girl longer than a week or two." Roscoe almost sounded worried. "Don't tell me you're getting serious about this one."

I shrugged casually, but a huge grin crept across my face despite myself. "What if I am?"

Martian's and Roscoe's mouths dropped open simultaneously.

"Aw, man!" Martian grumbled. "There go the big crowds of girls."

"Tell him, Raina," Roscoe urged. "Tell him this is the worst thing he can do to the band."

"Don't ask her," I said, laughing. "She's been

110

wanting me to do this forever. Right, Rain?"

"Right," she said, adjusting her keyboard.

Only for some reason, she didn't sound all that convinced.

After practice I asked Raina to stick around awhile. It seemed like years since I'd talked to her privately, and I wanted to hear her straight thoughts on everything that had happened. So we grabbed a couple of Cokes out of the fridge and headed up to my room. Raina lay back on my beanbag chair, her straight blond hair spread out against the navy vinyl like a feathery plume.

"Wow, Jase. We're actually going to Fourthfest!"

I smiled back at her. "Hard to believe, isn't it? Seems like just a few weeks ago we were running scales in Mr. Peabody's class. 'Pianissimo, boys and girls. Pianissimo,'" I said, waving my hands in the air and imitating Peabody's soft, shaky voice.

Raina cracked up. "Every time he said that, we thought he was saying a bad word. What dopes we were."

"And now we dopes are heading to the big stage!" I dropped down on my desk chair and whirled it around.

"Your parents must be pretty jazzed, huh?"

"My mom is. Dad's not exactly turning cart-wheels." I sighed and stared out my window toward the garage as if I could see into the future. "You know, Rain, you're probably the only person in the world who really understands what my music means to me."

"Oh, come on."

"It's true. Dad thinks it's a big nuisance. Mom's proud of me, but she just likes to see me happy. If I told her tomorrow I was giving it all up to go to dental school, she'd back me up with no questions asked. Roscoe and Martian don't get it either. They think I only care about becoming famous and getting lots of girls." I turned and faced Raina's sprawled form. "But you know me. You know this is all . . . part of me. Like you said."

"Yeah," she said softly, turning onto her side to look at me. "I do."

"I've wanted this for as long as I can remember. Heck, I've been writing songs since I was in kindergarten. Of course, back then they were all about flying in airplanes or accidentally dropping your ice-cream cone."

Raina laughed. "Now there's a blues tune for you."

I grinned and shook my head. It was hard to imagine those early stages of my dream—playing air guitar on tennis rackets and mouthing along to CDs in my room by myself. Somehow it seemed as though Raina had always been a part of it.

"You were the first person I ever showed my songs to," I told her thoughtfully. "And you took me seriously. You encouraged me." I walked over and sat down beside her, squeezing her hand. "I mean, you said it was because of me that we got

112

into Fourthfest—that it was my dream. But really, it's your doing. If it weren't for you, I would've never had the guts even to go after this."

Raina sat up slowly and stared at me intently. Her hair was kind of poufy and her dark eyes looked narrow and thoughtful. For an instant she seemed older, wiser, and prettier than I ever remembered her looking. It was weird, but it felt as though we were back in junior-high band class and I was the skinny dork with a mad crush on her.

Then suddenly she smirked and rolled her eyes, and the old Raina returned.

"Yeah, well, I just saw a good opportunity," she said, taking her hand from mine and using it to smooth down her hair. "I figured you could use another song-writer, and I wanted to share your millions."

"That reminds me," I said, standing up. "There's a reason I wanted you to stick around tonight."

"Oh? Why?"

I sat down on my bed and reached for my acoustic guitar. "I've been trying to write a song about Trudy—a real love song—but I keep getting stuck. Think you could help?"

She grimaced slightly. "I don't think so, Jase."

"Aw, come on. What is it, Rain? I get the feel-ing you aren't the least bit happy for me about Trudy."

Raina stood up and sighed. "It's not that," she said. "It's just that . . . it's late. We had a rough prac-tice. I'm not up for a songwriting session right now."

"Just help me with a good first verse. Please?" I asked, flashing her my hound-dog expression. "I was hoping to use it to impress her this weekend."

"You don't need to impress her with a song. You're Jason Lauderette." She smiled and poked me in the ribs. "If you can't win her over, she's not even alive—she's one of those New Orleans zombies we read about."

"Maybe," I said, chuckling. "But I still want to write a killer song before Fourthfest. Something with soul."

"Jase, you're thinking way too much about this soul thing." She shook her head and opened the door. "Quit trying so hard. Your songs were good enough to get us into Fourthfest, right?"

"*Our* songs," I corrected her. "We wrote them together."

Raina smiled faintly. "Yeah. We make a great team, don't we?" she said quietly.

"We always have," I told her.

"Right." She stared at me for a moment, her eyes sharp and penetrating. Then she turned to leave. "'Night, Jase," she said.

A vague feeling of uncertainty came over me as I watched her disappear down the stairway. Something was up with Raina. For the first time ever, I just couldn't read her, and I had no idea why. As excited as I was about Trudy and Fourthfest, I couldn't help feeling pretty bummed as I thought about it. What if I was losing my best friend?

Nine

IT WAS A quarter to ten on Saturday, almost the end of our set, and Trudy still hadn't shown up at the café. My panic grew with each passing minute. Where could she be?

To top it off, we were playing terribly. Or, more specifically, *I* was. I was forgetting lines, dropping chords, losing the tempo, and just generally doing horribly.

"Jason!" Raina hissed at me in between songs. "Will you please stop thinking about you-know-who and get with it? We've got a show to do."

"Just lay off, okay? It's not going that badly."

Roscoe coughed significantly, smirking beneath his hand. For a few seconds I hated him. And I dreaded the teasing he and Martian would subject me to if I was stood up.

"Besides," I continued in a loud whisper, "no one seems to mind."

115

That was true, actually. The usual layer of girls that flanked the stage hardly seemed to notice my flubs. And when I announced at the beginning of the show that we'd made Fourthfest, the crowd had gone totally nuts. They cheered for what seemed like a whole hour and chanted, "Fourth-*fest!* Fourth-*fest!* Fourth-*fest!* " between each song.

At the time it had felt incredible, but now I barely felt like making eye contact with any of the fans. As the bar clock's menacing face revealed how obviously, terribly, inexcusably late Trudy was getting to be, it was all I could do to hold on to the guitar.

There must be some explanation, I thought. *Trudy could've been in an accident and had to go to the hospital. Or maybe she fell deathly ill—or got stuck in an old mine shaft.* A hundred theories raced through my mind, but none of them made me feel any better.

Finally our gig ended—an hour and a half that had felt more like a geological era. I morosely thanked the crowd and started packing up my equipment.

Martian approached me as I angrily slammed my guitar case shut.

"Um, Jason?" he asked. "You're not going to play like that at Fourthfest, are you?"

I glared at him with such contempt, I wouldn't have been surprised to see his glasses grow foggy and his hair curl up. He backed up slowly without saying another word.

Raina, who'd witnessed the entire exchange, walked over and put a hand on my arm. "Hey, Jase," she said softly. "Are you okay?"

The look of pity on her face only made me fume with anger. I didn't want anyone—not even my closest friends—feeling sorry for me.

"I'm fine, all right?" I snapped.

I tore my arm away from Raina and stalked over to the front counter. By that time the crowd had already cleared out to head to Tony's party, so luckily no one bothered me.

"Could I have a Coke, Sylvester?" I shut my eyes and exhaled slowly. "Please?"

"Sure thing." He poured it the way I liked it, with lots of shaved ice and a lemon wedge on the side. Then he just stood behind the counter, quietly drying glasses and setting them on the blue plastic rack beside him.

Maybe it was the caffeine. Maybe I was hypnotized by Sylvester's steady, mechanical motions. Or maybe it was the fact that he *didn't* ask me what was wrong. But I was on my third soda when I heard myself say, "This is probably the worst night of my life."

"Now, you're just being too hard on yourself," he remarked as he wiped out the inside of a tea glass. "Every musician has a bad night now and then."

"I guess," I muttered, feeling a sharp pang of guilt. I couldn't believe I'd let a girl interfere with my music. That had never happened before. I didn't know which was worse: the fact that Trudy had stood me up or the fact that I was so depressed that she had stood me up.

By the time I finished my drink, I felt pretty bad about the way I'd yelled at the band—especially at Raina. I decided to apologize to her before she loaded up and left. Maybe we could head over to Tony's together, or just blow it off completely and go hang out at my house. If anyone could cheer me up, it was her.

"Thanks, Sylvester," I said, fishing a crumpled dollar bill from my pocket.

He held up a large, callused hand. "No, no. It's on the house, son. I'm always glad to help a fellow guitar man."

I gave him a small smile, then scanned the place for Raina. I spotted her across the room, winding up her microphone cord. I began to head in her direction, forming what I hoped was an appropriately apologetic expression on my face. Then suddenly a hand reached out from nowhere and whirled me around.

"Hey! Am I too late? Has the party already started without us?" Trudy stood in front of me looking completely cheerful, with not a trace of remorse on her perfect features.

"Are you *too late?*" I repeated incredulously. "The gig's over. You missed the whole thing."

Trudy looked confused. "What? Are you mad or something? We were supposed to meet here before we went to the party. You said nothing about actually watching your show."

My head spun as I stared back at her. "Why would I ask you to the party and not want you here for the show? That doesn't make sense."

She shrugged, tucking her sleek dark hair behind her ears. "I don't know. I mean, this gig is like your job, right? I figured it was a meet-me-after-work sort of thing. Sorry if I misunderstood."

I blinked back at her, at a loss for words. "This isn't just a job," I said finally, my voice rising slightly. "This is important to me. It's—it's part of who I am."

"Look, I said I was sorry." A hurt expression came over her face. "What more do you want me to say? Besides," she continued, "I couldn't have come here earlier even if I wanted to. I got a long-distance call from Mother, all the way from France."

I tried not to let the phrase "even if I wanted to" get on my nerves. "A *two-hour* phone call?" I chided gently.

"Well, no. But I had to get ready. I wanted to look good for you." She took a step back so I could admire the full view.

She looked better than ever in a short, dark red dress that was barely bigger than a handkerchief. The only things holding it up were her bust and two spaghetti-thin straps that tied around her graceful neck.

All my anger disappeared in an instant. Hormones are powerful that way.

"You look beautiful," I told her, smiling.

She grinned back at me, and her green eyes glittered like my mom's emerald ring. I was a goner.

"Great," she said. "Okay, then. Time to make a grand entrance at the social event of the summer." She twirled around on her platform sandals and took a step toward the front door.

"Wait!" I said, grabbing her hand. "Before we go, there's something I want to tell you. Some really great news."

"Oh? What's that?"

I beamed at her, already anticipating her reaction. "My band's going to be playing in this year's Fourthfest!" I calmly waited for my congratulatory hug and possible kiss.

She nodded. "Huh. That's great," she said. "What's Fourthfest?"

I tried not to let my rush of disappointment get me too down. How would she know what Fourthfest was? "It's this big music festival they have out here every summer. A real blowout. It's . . . well, I'll tell you about it on the way to Tony's."

"Excellent. Well, let's go," she ordered, then trotted toward the door. Her stride was brisk, even in heels, and I marveled at the way her silky dress bounced and swirled around the lines of her body.

Trudy was halfway across the room when she turned and looked back to where I was standing, stupidly staring after her. "Come on, big shot," she said with a laugh. "Your public awaits." She ran back over to me, slipped her arm through mine, and tugged me toward the exit.

"Right," I replied with a smile. "Mustn't disappoint the fans."

Then I remembered Raina. I glanced over my shoulder to look for her, but she wasn't anywhere in sight. The place was empty.

Oh, well, I thought. *I'll catch her at Tony's and apologize there. She'll understand.*

Suddenly I couldn't wait to arrive at the party. News of Fourthfest was circulating through the masses, and the most incredible girl in the world would be there beside me.

This was going to be a night to remember. I could feel it.

"Oh, my God!" Brenda shrieked for the hundredth time. "You guys are going to be huge. I just know it!"

"Think about all the famous people you'll get to meet," Junie added.

"But don't forget your buddies back home after you guys have become superstars," Tony Brewer said, elbowing me in the ribs.

Trudy stood at my side, smiling and sipping a drink. She wasn't saying much, but then, she wasn't being given much of a chance to. Since our arrival we'd been mobbed by people wanting to know the scoop on Fourthfest.

I was flying high. Having so many excited fans come up and congratulate me made our success sink in a little more. It was almost unreal, as if I'd jumped into one of my daydreams.

The only thing that kept it from being absolutely perfect was Raina. I'd been keeping an eye out for her since we'd arrived, but I still hadn't seen her. I wondered if she could be avoiding me after the way I'd snapped at her. Thinking about it made me feel like a total jerk.

Roscoe and Martian stood in the dining room surrounded by a group of fans. Maybe they knew where she was.

"I'm going to the refreshment table for a sec," I whispered to Trudy. "Can I get you something?"

"No, thanks," she said, smiling weakly. She looked a little bored, and I wondered if all the commotion over Fourthfest was wearing her down. I told myself I'd pay more attention to her after I checked on Raina. Maybe even go for a romantic stroll in the backyard.

I walked up to Roscoe and tapped him on the shoulder. "Have you seen Raina anywhere?" I asked.

"Nope," he replied, shaking his head. "But I saw her car when I pulled up. She's around here somewhere."

"She's probably surrounded by half the football team—that's why we can't see her," Martian added.

"Hey, I noticed your girlfriend finally showed," Roscoe commented, drawing out the word *girlfriend*. "Man, she looks hot!"

"Where?" Martian asked. "Where is she?"

I quickly scanned the living room. "Over there," I said, pointing. Trudy stood in the far corner talking with Tony's older brother, Nelson. I caught her eye and waved. She smiled and nodded back at me.

"Whoa!" Martian exclaimed. "If you were ever going to get serious about a girl, Jase, Trudy's definitely the type. She looks like a supermodel."

"Yeah," I said, keeping my eyes on Trudy. She tilted back her head, laughing at something Nelson said. Her smile seemed to light up the room, and the ends of her dark hair grazed her bare shoulders. She was so beautiful. In a way, I felt the same way about her as I felt about making Fourthfest—that she was almost too good to be true.

Just then I caught sight of Raina walking through the kitchen. "There she is," I said. I pushed my way past the other guys and snuck up behind her. "Yo!" I exclaimed, squeezing her rib cage.

"Aaugh!" she screamed, and whirled around. "God, Jase! You just about scared the pee out of me!"

"Is this party great or what?" I asked. "Everyone is talking about us."

"Yeah. They sure seem thrilled." She turned and smiled at me. "Glad to see *you're* in a better mood."

"Um, yeah . . ." I leaned in closer and lowered my voice. "Hey, Rain, I'm sorry about the way I acted back at the Post. I was—"

"Distracted. I know," she finished for me. She sighed and shook her head. "I've never seen a girl get to you like this."

"I know! That's the thing—there's just something about her. I guess it makes me a little crazy."

"I'll say," Raina replied, a shadow falling over her eyes. "So why was she so late tonight?"

I shrugged. "It was just a misunderstanding. It's all worked out now." As I spoke, I looked around for Trudy. She was still talking to Nelson in the corner. As she listened to him, she slowly twisted her left foot into the plush carpeting. I figured it was a gesture of impatience and felt guilty for having left her for so long, but I found it extremely alluring. Actually, just about every movement she made was alluring to me.

"Hey, Jason," Roscoe called as he walked up next to us. "You'd better go reclaim your woman before someone else does."

Martian trotted up behind him. "Yeah. I think Nelson Brewer is putting the moves on her."

"Yeah, right," I said, rolling my eyes. "Trudy's not like that. She's very mature."

"*And* very hot," Martian added.

"Funny, I was thinking she's probably cold, wearing a dress like that on a breezy night," Raina commented.

I shoved her arm playfully. "Aw, come on." I smiled. "You know, *you* should wear outfits like that to our gigs. It would be totally sexy."

"And totally impractical," she retorted. "If I showed up in something that skimpy on gig night, then you guys would have to set up all my equipment."

"Well, I think it's a great idea," Roscoe said. "Think how good it would be for business. Guys would storm the place. Sylvester's profits would double!"

"Ugh," Raina groaned. "The air stinks of testosterone around here. If you'll excuse me, I'm going to find Casey and Renee." She slid past us and disappeared into the milling crowd.

"Martian and I are headed up to the roof of the carport," Roscoe said to me. "They're setting up empty bottles and knocking them down with Mr. Brewer's bowling ball. You want to grab your supermodel and join us?"

"No, thanks," I replied. "You boys run along and have fun. Trudy and I need some quality time. Alone."

The two of them exchanged knowing glances and took off.

Now it was finally time to grab Trudy and see about that romantic stroll. My palms started to sweat at the mere thought of finally kissing her. It was quite possible that this night was going to surpass any fantasy I'd ever had.

I looked over to where Trudy had been standing a moment earlier, but she wasn't there anymore. A quick search of the kitchen and dining room didn't turn her up either. I figured she'd probably headed to the rest room.

I glanced down at my watch and realized that I had only an hour before Trudy needed to be home. I had to find her right away. I'd already spent too much of the evening talking to other people. Now it was time to focus on her—on *us.*

I'd no sooner taken two steps in the direction of the bathroom when a hand clamped down on my shoulder. *What now?* I thought, exasperated.

It was Raina. "Jason, I need to talk to you," she said in a solemn whisper.

"It can wait."

"But it's really important."

"Later, okay? I have to find Trudy."

"Don't you 'later' me!" she scolded. "It so happens that Trudy is what I need to talk to you about. I . . . uh . . . I know where she is."

"Great," I said, turning around. "Where is she?"

Raina bit her lip. Her eyes darted to the floor.

"Well?" I asked, growing impatient. "Where is she?"

"She's with Nelson," Raina said quickly. "She left on the back of his motorcycle about five minutes ago."

"What?" I could feel my face growing pale. My knees felt as though they might buckle. "You're joking, right?"

Raina put her hand on my arm. "I'm sorry, Jase, but I'm not."

A cold wave washed over me. *No,* I thought. *There's no way this is happening.* But one look into Raina's eyes told me she was telling the truth, as impossible as it seemed.

I felt nauseated. I felt hurt. I felt angry. I felt . . .

I felt as though about a hundred curious stares were pointed in my direction, and I could hear their muffled whispers.

Without looking into anyone else's eyes I booked it—through the living room and out the front door, into the cool moonlight. Raina ran after me, but I was already slamming the van into fourth gear by the time she got outside.

Ten

"JASON! TELEPHONE!" MY mother called out.

I moaned from my sprawled position on my bed and sat up. "Take a message!" I shouted, then slumped back down.

After Trudy had blown me off Saturday night, I'd gone back to my room and hadn't left it for two days. I wouldn't accept any calls or visitors, explaining to my mom that I felt really sick. She had no problem believing that, since I stayed in bed all the time and barely ate a thing.

I just couldn't deal with the current reality of my life. News of the way Trudy had ditched me for Nelson had probably circulated faster than a rabbit in heat, and I knew I couldn't handle everyone's stares and false sympathy. It was better to hide out and not even think about it.

Ironically, though, it was all I thought about. For forty-eight hours I'd done nothing but replay the party in my head—only I was no closer to understanding it now than I was then.

How could Trudy do this to me? I asked myself over and over. It just wasn't fair. Here I'd finally found someone special, someone I could see myself with for a long time, but I'd ended up getting royally blown off on the second date—in front of the entire town!

"Jason." My mom appeared in the doorway. "Pick up the phone, sweetie. It's for you."

I turned my face to the wall. "I don't want to talk to anyone right now."

"They're saying it's important," she added.

Important? An amazing girl had screeched out of my life on the back of a Harley-Davidson. What could possibly be important just then? "Please just take a message," I mumbled.

"But it's some woman calling about Fourthfest."

Fourthfest? Oh, yeah. *That* was important. "Okay," I said, jumping off the bed and reaching for my cordless phone. "I've got it." I waited until my mom left the room and hung up the extension before I cleared my throat and said, "Hello?"

"Don't hang up," came a familiar voice on the other end.

"Raina! What did you do? Lie to my mom?"

"Hey, I didn't know what else to do," she said. "I'm worried about you. I've called, like, four hundred times, and your mother keeps saying you're sick."

"I am sick. Sick of life. Sick of people. Sick of

130

everything," I muttered. "So if you'll excuse me—"

"Wait!"

Here it comes, I thought. *The pity.* I placed my finger over the on-off button, ready to push it as soon as Raina mentioned the party. "What is it?" I snapped.

"I was just wondering . . . why did you pick up the phone just now?" she asked.

"Huh?" Her question threw me. "Because you lied and I thought it was about Fourthfest. Duh."

"Well, then, you aren't exactly sick of everything, are you? You're not giving up on Fourthfest, right?"

She had me there. But what was the point? "Of course not," I replied. "You know how important that is to me."

"Then why don't you meet me for lunch at the Post tomorrow? We need to talk about the upcoming show and plan some rehearsals and stuff."

"I don't think so, Rain," I mumbled.

"Jason! We have a little over a week to prepare!" she exclaimed. "Plus we've got that out-of-town gig in Monroe two days from now."

She was right. We really did need to work. "Okay," I said, giving in. "But can't you come here instead of me going there?"

"Uh-uh. Sorry. Sylvester really needs me to work all day. It's lunch break or nothing."

I sighed into the receiver.

"Come on, Jase. Can't you crawl out of your cave long enough to have lunch?"

I was amazed at how matter-of-fact she sounded—as if we were just making casual plans, without any mention of the huge disaster I'd gone through two nights earlier. Deep down I knew she was only trying to get me out of the house, but I was grateful she wasn't forcing me to talk about anything yet. Plus just hearing her voice made me feel a little better.

I decided to go along with it.

"All right," I said. "I'll be there. But only for a little while, okay?"

"Don't worry," she said. "It'll be quick and painless."

Quick and painless? I thought as I hung up the phone. *I sure hope so. Because I don't think I can handle any more pain.*

I scanned the parking lot of the Scratchin' Post to see if I recognized any of the cars. Raina's blue Honda was there, as well as Sylvester's ancient white Cadillac, but nothing else looked familiar. With a heavy sigh I stepped inside.

The place seemed changed somehow, more dismal. Had it been only two days earlier that Trudy and I had left for the party arm in arm? It felt more like months ago. There was the wooden platform that my band performed on regularly. It looked small and desolate—just the way I felt. There was the front counter, where Sylvester had poured me my Coke. I should have stayed there all evening. Then maybe I wouldn't have suffered the humiliation that came later.

"Hello, son," Sylvester greeted as I straddled a stool at the counter. "Why the long face? You got the blues?"

"No. Just girl problems," I mumbled.

Sylvester laughed and shook his head. "That's the worst kind of blues. You ought to talk it out with your guitar or"—he pointed to Raina, who was busy busing a table—"a lovely lady."

"Okay if she takes a break, Sylvester?" I asked.

"No problem, son. You two take all the time you need."

I waved to Raina and sat down in a far booth, facing the back wall. She soon joined me with a couple of bowls of fresh étouffée.

"Glad you came," she said, her eyes searching my face. "How are you?"

"I'm cool."

"Good."

She waited for me to say something more. I didn't.

"Well, then," she continued in a cheerful yet businesslike tone, "what do you think about our Fourthfest set? I personally would like to open it with something up-tempo, like 'Cattin' Around' or 'Fever Pitch,' but then I know you like to save those for a big finish. So how about we . . ."

Her voice trailed off in my mind as I thought back to Saturday night. Talk about a big finish. Things had started so perfectly. How had they ended so disastrously? It was totally unreal—as if I'd slipped into a negative universe or something.

". . . of course, Roscoe will probably be bouncing all over the stage," Raina continued. "And Martian might pass out as soon as we're introduced. Maybe we could periodically slap him out of his stupor, or get some sort of happy medicine for him. . . ."

Medicine . . . What was it that Shelly had said to me outside the movie theater? That one day I'd get a taste of my own medicine? Maybe she'd worked some voodoo on me.

"Jase? Jason? Hello-o?" Raina sang out, waving her spoon in front of me. "Are you with me?"

"Yeah, I'm sorry. I was just . . ." I sighed and stared down at my uneaten étouffée. Suddenly I couldn't stand it any longer. "I feel like such an idiot!" I yelled, slamming my fist down on the table. "How could she ditch me like that in front of everyone?"

Raina stared at me in silence for a moment. Then she said, "I don't know, Jase."

"I tried so hard for her to like me. I mean, Trudy was never falling all over me the way other girls usually do. But I liked that. It made me sort of . . . I don't know . . . respect her more." I sighed wearily and rested my forehead in my hands. "I really thought she was special, Rain. And I thought we were starting something special. But I was nothing to her."

"Don't say that," Raina murmured.

"Then why'd she do it? Why'd she make me think she was into me if she wasn't? Didn't she consider my feelings?" I lifted my head and stared right into Raina's dark eyes, hoping for some sort of explanation.

To my surprise, Raina had a small smirk on her face.

"What? What's so funny?" I demanded.

"I'm sorry," she said, concern returning to her features. "It's just that, well, I've heard so many girls use those same words when talking about you."

My mouth dropped open at the comparison. "That's not fair. I've never dumped anyone like that. I've never showed up at a party with one girl and left with another."

Raina nodded. "True. You've never done anything *that* bad. But face it, Jase. You did lead a lot of girls on. In a way, you sort of got what you deserved."

For a brief moment I just stared at her, my hands tightening into fists. Whose side was she on, anyway? Eventually my vocal cords reactivated. "Funny," I snapped. "I thought I was talking to my best friend."

"I *am* your friend!" she protested. "I just think it's time you faced reality. Look," she added, leaning in closer to me, "this may surprise you, but you've hurt a lot of girls—probably as badly as Trudy hurt you. And what's so frustrating is that you never seem to care." She fell back into her seat, shaking her head. "Sometimes I wish you'd go back to being that nice, shy guy in my junior-high band class."

Now she had me totally confused. She preferred me as a dork? "What? How can you say that?"

"You used to be so sweet," Raina told me. "I mean, I know you're still a great guy, but I can't stand watching the way you treat girls. It's like you turn into this inconsiderate jerk and you don't even realize it."

I shook my head, anger building inside me. "I can't believe you're actually lecturing me right now," I barked. "Why are you acting like I'm the villain? *I'm* the one who just got his heart stomped on. *I'm* the one who just lost the greatest girl I've ever met in my life."

"As far as I can see, the only thing you've lost is some snotty girl who's obviously been sniffing hair spray too long," Raina said, wrinkling her nose. "I'm sorry she hurt you, but you're better off. Maybe now you'll see how dangerous it is to mess with people's feelings."

"You're not sorry. *I'm* the one who's sorry," I muttered as I scooted out of the booth and stood up. "I'm sorry I ever came here to talk to you. I'm sorry I thought you'd actually care about what I'm going through."

"I do care," she said, reaching for my arm. "Come on. Don't go. We really should talk."

"I'm through talking to you." I wrenched my arm out of her grasp and stalked through the restaurant as fast as my rage could propel me.

I had thought things couldn't get any worse, but I was wrong. Way wrong.

First Trudy, now Raina. Suddenly I couldn't trust anyone.

My head throbbed as I stepped out into the broiling sunshine. I didn't want beautiful weather just then. I wanted it to be cloudy and rainy, with maybe a fierce tornado or two. Since the universe seemed to be working against me lately, it could at least provide a fitting backdrop.

I was a total mess. My anger at Raina had added a new layer to the pain and confusion that had been occupying space inside me—not to mention the monumental self-pity. I couldn't believe how hard she'd been on me. What good was a best friend if she turned on you when you needed her most?

Now I had no one. No girlfriend. No best friend. And I was still too freaked out to face our fans. Thank goodness our next gig was out of town. Until then, all I wanted to do was crawl back into bed and avoid all human contact.

I walked over to the far edge of the parking lot, where I'd parked my van, when suddenly I spotted a familiar red gleam across the street. I should have ignored it—but I didn't.

It was Trudy's car. Only that wasn't the worst of it. Just at that moment Trudy herself was coming out of the coffee shop across the street nuzzled in the crook of Nelson Brewer's right arm. I stood there watching like a paralyzed masochist as they leaned against Trudy's car and kissed.

She never kissed me, I thought.

My heart felt as though it were sore and bleeding, but I couldn't turn away. When their lips finally parted—which seemed to take a few lunar cycles—Nelson hopped onto his motorcycle and drove off.

Suddenly a raw, bristly anger coursed through me, and my face probably turned the color of Trudy's Miata.

It's not fair, I thought. *She never even gave me a chance.*

I should've just turned and left, but I didn't. Before I realized what I was doing, I'd crossed the street and marched up to Trudy just as she was unlocking her car.

"Gee, I'd have thought you'd be riding on the back of his bike," I muttered through clenched teeth.

Trudy whirled around to face me. "What are you doing here?" she asked.

"I came for an explanation. I think I deserve to know what's going on." A gnawing pain was working its way through my gut, but somehow I managed to keep my voice steady.

She sighed impatiently. "What do you mean, what's going on?"

"I mean," I said, folding my arms across my chest, "what's going on with you and Nelson?"

"*That's* none of your business."

"It sure was my business on Saturday when you took off with him and left me behind!" I yelled.

"Oh, so you noticed," she commented sarcastically. "I thought you were too busy signing autographs."

The bitterness in her voice stung me. I looked into her beautiful face, searching for some evidence of her feelings for me, but her features remained cold and blank.

No! I refused to accept it. After everything we'd gone through—the secret smiles, the shared jokes, the promises of having "plenty of time"—there *had* to be something there between us still.

"I don't understand. How could you totally blow me off like that?" I demanded. "We had something really great going, and you just threw it away. Why?" My words tapered off into a whine. By that point I'd completely self-destructed. All efforts to remain cool had shattered beyond repair.

She shut her eyes and sighed again. "Look, that's just how it is. Sometimes things don't work out," she said, talking to me as if I were an annoying five-year-old. "I thought you of all people would understand that."

"What does that mean?"

"Don't you remember? At the movie theater? We laughed at how annoying your ex-girlfriend was, and now here you are sounding just like her."

My mouth fell open. *Wait . . . That can't be. . . .*

"But . . . but that's different," I muttered.

"No, it isn't," she said, opening her car door and climbing in. "The only thing different is that it's happening to you. It was fun, Jason, but now it's over."

She moved to shut her door, but I stopped it with my hand. "No! It wasn't just fun—it was more than that. It was real. I could *feel* it."

"You felt what you wanted to feel," she said flatly. "That's not real." Then she reached over and slammed her car door shut, narrowly missing my fingers.

I stood and watched as her car disappeared down Canal Street, too miserable to move.

How could she be so cold? So cruel?

After all the dating around, I'd finally found the perfect girl for me—and she couldn't care less. If it hadn't hurt so much, I would have laughed at the sick irony of it all.

But I didn't think I'd ever feel like laughing again.

Eleven

MONROE IS ONLY fifty miles away from Tallulah, but as we drove there in my stuffy van the next day, it felt as though it were in a different time zone.

"Jase, do you have to drive so fast?" Raina asked, gripping the passenger-side door handle as I accelerated to pass another car.

"Do you want to make the gig on time?" I snapped.

"Well, yes, but—"

"Then I have to drive fast." I clenched my jaw and resumed downshifting into passing gear. Actually, we still had plenty of time to make it to the dance hall that had booked us for the evening, but I wasn't going to tell Raina that. As far as I was concerned, I wasn't going to tell Raina anything anymore. She'd only turn on me anyway.

"All right," she muttered, slouching back in her

seat. "Then *you* can pay for the speeding ticket."

"Fine!" I told her.

"Fine!" she yelled back.

In the rearview mirror, I could see Roscoe and Martian exchange wary looks. They weren't saying much on this drive either. I figured Raina must have terrorized them into avoiding all discussion of Trudy or Tony Brewer's party, and for that I was grateful. But the silence that enveloped us as we cruised along the highway was just as blatantly awkward. And left with only my own thoughts for company, I was beginning to lose it a little.

I couldn't stop thinking about Trudy and the cold way she'd blown me off to my face. It made me feel totally unworthy, as if I'd slid down the evolutionary scale and turned into a garden slug overnight. I had been so *positive* she was the one for me, only to end up stabbed through the heart. Just as I'd been positive Raina would always be there for me as a friend.

This is bogus! I raged inwardly. *I didn't do anything wrong, and now everyone's treating me like dirt! I don't need them. I don't need anybody.*

Of course, I *did* need to get through our gig that night somehow. And as much as I wanted to pull over to the side of the highway and dump the rest of the band, I knew I couldn't. I just had to hang on for a few more hours. Then I could go home and be safe from everyone's criticism and pity.

Sucking in my breath, I tried desperately to shut down all unnecessary thought, compacting all the

142

hurt and anger into a tidy package and burying it inside me. I wanted to become Jason Lauderette, human robot—impervious to pain and dependent on no one. But even as I managed to push down my stress, I knew it wouldn't last. Somewhere deep inside me, my ball of suppressed emotions started ticking.

"Look! It's the turnoff!" Martian exclaimed as I drove past a Monroe exit sign. Beside him, Roscoe bounced excitedly in his seat.

If I'd been allowing myself to experience feelings, I probably would have jumped for joy too. This gig really was a big deal for us. With the exception of a late-night party out on the Scofields' farm the past spring, we'd never played outside Tallulah's city limits. After Sylvester had hired us at the Post, I'd decided to put out a promotional flyer to local businesses, advertising us as professional musicians for hire. Somehow a copy fell into the hands of a Monroe club owner and he called up and booked us, explaining that his usual band wasn't available. We'd get one hundred dollars and a chance to widen our audience. And compared to Tallulah, Monroe was a bustling metropolis.

"Man, we're gonna blow this town away!" Roscoe sang out as we headed into Monroe's downtown area. "I bet their local sounds can't compare at all!"

"Hey, yeah. Maybe we'll be so much better than the regular group, this guy will hire us on permanently," Martian said.

I almost allowed myself a smile. Roscoe was right. From what I'd heard, our band was the best of its kind in northern Louisiana. If our gig that night was a success, maybe it could help me regain my sense of control. That wouldn't be so bad.

I slowed the van to a crawl and squinted at the road signs.

"Which street is it?" Raina asked.

"Louisville," I muttered.

"And where is that? Is it far?"

I shrugged. "I don't know. He said it was in the main part of town, where we are now. We'll find it."

She sighed and reached for a map on the floorboard. "You know, we could always check—"

"I *said* we'll find it." Obviously Raina had no faith in me, and I could feel my fury start to reveal itself. I closed my eyes briefly and took a deep breath, forcing it back down.

A half a mile later we finally found Louisville Avenue. "See?" I said, making the turn. "I knew what I was doing. The club should be somewhere along the next block." We crept along the street, looking at the row of old yellow-brick buildings. We were already past the joint before Raina noticed the faded, vine-covered sign over the doorway.

"Joe's Depot. Isn't that the place?"

"That's right." I hung a sharp U-turn, causing our equipment to slide to the opposite side of the van. "Show time!"

We drove through the crater-infested parking lot

and backed up to the rear entrance. An older man wearing a black suit and an old-time shoestring tie met us outside.

"Howdy! I'm Joe Sachs. Are you all the Bonkheads?"

"Bankheads," I corrected. "Hello, Mr. Sachs. I'm Jason Lauderette. We spoke on the phone."

Mr. Sachs scratched his head and peered at us as we opened up the van's side door and began unloading our stuff. "Forgive me, but I have to say, you all are a lot younger than I expected. Have y'all done a lot of these shows?"

"Oh, yeah," I assured him. "We're regulars at the Scratchin' Post Café back in Tallulah. Don't worry, sir. I assure you, we're professionals."

"Well, all righty, then. Feel free to set up your equipment however you like. People will be showing up before too long."

Inside, Joe's Depot looked like an ancient, stripped-down warehouse. Our footsteps echoed off the concrete floor, the gray cinder-block walls, and the long steel beams that hung from the ceiling like a cage ready to be lowered. Mr. Sachs gestured to a tiny wooden platform along the back wall of the building, referring to it as the "stage." The rotting boards creaked as we weighted it with our heavy gear, and when I tried to plug in my rig, a small shower of sparks leaped from the outlet.

"This place gives me the creeps," Martian mumbled.

"Yeah," Roscoe said, nodding. "I feel like we've

stumbled onto the set of a Batman movie."

"Get over it, guys. What'd you expect? A Vegas nightclub?" I muttered, dusting off my jeans. The show was the only thing going for me right then, and I wasn't going to let them ruin it for me.

"Um . . . who are those people?" Raina asked, pointing to a group of people who had come through the front door.

"Zombies!" Martian gasped.

"Evil clones?" Roscoe suggested.

It really was almost unearthly looking. Several couples were milling around on the open floor. They all looked older, about the age of my grandparents, and they were all dressed the same. The men had on suits with the same sort of string tie Mr. Sachs was sporting, and the women were all wearing white blouses and short skirts that poufed out at a radius of two feet around them.

"Um . . . Jason?" Raina said. "Is the fashion totally different here in Monroe, or are they dressed for what I think they're dressed for?"

"Why would these people be coming to see us?" Roscoe asked. "They all look like—"

"Square dancers!" finished Martian.

I blinked and shook my head as if I could make the assembled crowd disappear. "No, it can't be. There must be some mistake."

There was.

Raina put on her best public-relations face and walked over to talk to Mr. Sachs. In a few minutes she returned, scowling and waving a paper in her hand. "Well, Jase. Thanks to your twisted grammar, we've been confused with a square-dance band."

"What?" I could feel the knot of emotion inside me start to unravel. "But . . . how?"

She held up a copy of the promotional flyer I'd put out. Someone, Mr. Sachs most likely, had circled the phrases "foot-tapping music," "distinctly upbeat, southern sound," and the slogan I'd printed across the bottom: *The Bankheads—the best band to call your next gathering.*

"Don't you see?" she asked, pointing. "'*Call* your next gathering'? Square-dance calling?"

"But it was supposed to read 'to call *for* your next gathering,'" I explained, my voice becoming loud and distressed-sounding. "It's a typo."

Raina shrugged. "Well, he knows that now. He was very nice about it, luckily, and said he'd still pay us, since we've come all this way and he never mentioned the specific music he wanted when he booked us."

"Aw, man! This is just perfect!" I pounded my fist against the rickety platform, causing a slight seismic motion that rattled the equipment. *What's happening? Can't anything go right in my life?* Any more surprises and they'd be carting me off in a straitjacket.

"So . . . uh . . . what do you want us to do, Jason? Should we break down our stuff?" Martian asked, eyeing me tentatively.

"Hey, maybe we could wing it," suggested Roscoe. He pantomimed holding a microphone and sang in a twangy voice, "Grab your partner, do-si-do, throw her in the air and go."

"Stop!" I hollered, slumping onto the stage. "It's not funny. We've driven all this way and set up our things and now what? Are we going to play rock-and-roll music for *this* crowd?"

"Why not?" Raina asked, her eyes determined and focused. "We're professionals, aren't we? We're not going to back down from a gig just because of some . . . minor confusion."

"Don't give me that!" Now I was really, really starting to lose it. The last thing I needed was a lecture from Raina. "We're leaving and that's that."

"Jason!" She stepped up to face me. "Will you stop moping and think about the band for a change? We won't get paid unless we play! Besides, we should all have a say in whether we go or not—not just you!"

I narrowed my eyes at her, wishing that for once she wouldn't be so *right* all the time. I sighed. "Okay, fine. Martian? Roscoe? What do you guys want to do?"

They eyed each other hesitatingly.

"Um . . . I'd actually kind of like to play," Roscoe said.

"Yeah," Martian agreed. "Why not?"

I looked from Roscoe and Martian to Raina again, glaring intensely. What did I expect? They were all against me. The whole universe was against me. "Fine," I replied. "What do I know? I'm useless. A total wasteoid. Why should my feelings matter at all?" I stomped onto the stage and picked up my guitar while the rest of them stood below, eyeing me cautiously. "Well?" I shouted. "Come on! If we're going to play, let's play!"

They quietly walked onstage and began tuning their instruments.

"Jase," Raina whispered, "maybe you should calm down. Everything's going to be fine."

"Maybe you should quit telling me how to live my life," I growled through clenched teeth. I didn't mean to sound so vicious, but I couldn't help it. Why did she always have the power to make me feel like such a jerk?

"Hey! I was just trying to help," she said, sounding hurt.

I ignored her and walked away. I had nothing further to say—not that she would understand me anyway. Raina and I had been so close for so long. But now, even though she was right beside me, it felt as though she were thousands of miles away.

A half hour later we were in the van, driving back to Tallulah.

"See? I told you we shouldn't play," I grumbled, gripping the steering wheel as if I were trying to crush it.

"Will you get over it already?" Raina said. "It wasn't that bad. In fact, it started out better than I thought it would."

"Whatever. Not only was that the worst gig

we've ever done," I continued ranting, "it was also the shortest."

"I'm sorry," Roscoe moaned from the backseat. "I'm really, really sorry."

"It's okay, Roscoe," Raina said, twisting around in her seat. "Don't listen to him."

I flashed her the angriest look I could conjure up and turned back to the road. The next few minutes passed in total silence. As I drove, the evening's events replayed in my head like a nightmare.

Raina was right about the gig's starting off okay. After our first song, two-thirds of the square dancers left, but I was surprised at how many stuck around, some of them even getting up to dance to our music. It was kind of funny to watch them shake their rear ends and tap along in their pointy, heavy-soled shoes. Even old Mr. Sachs was clapping and whistling. After a while, I started to get into it despite myself—not that I would admit that to Raina.

But two songs later it was all over. Roscoe tried to make one of his fancy jumps and ended up crashing into one of the steel beams overhead, knocking him flat and effectively ending our set.

"How're you feeling, by the way?" Raina asked Roscoe.

"I'm okay," he mumbled pitifully. "The ice pack is helping, but I'll probably have a Wile E. Coyote–type lump on the top of my head."

"That means you'll be even taller," Martian said with a chuckle.

"I don't think it's all that funny," I said. "He could've broken his neck."

Raina sighed and threw up her hands. "Will you relax? He's fine. A little loopy, maybe, but then Roscoe wasn't all that clearheaded to begin with."

"Well, we certainly came across as professionals tonight," I muttered.

"I'm sorry," Roscoe said again.

"It's not your fault," Raina told him. "Jason's just being a jerk."

"Sing a new song, Raina," I seethed. "We've all heard that one." So now everything was my fault, according to Raina. It was my fault the gig was a joke. My fault Roscoe almost lobotomized himself. My fault my girlfriend turned on me. My fault there was war, disease, and starvation in the world.

I drove up to Roscoe's house and waited as he stumbled out of the van, one hand holding the ice pack and the other leaning on Martian like a human crutch. I was relieved when Martian volunteered to stay and explain everything to Roscoe's parents. I probably couldn't have kept my cool.

After Raina and I saw them disappear safely inside, we drove to the Scratchin' Post. Sylvester had loaned us a backup speaker for the set and had given us a key so we could return it.

I backed the van up to the rear door and slid the rig out onto the ground. Just as I was about to haul it upright, Raina appeared at my side and bent down to pick up one end.

"Get back in the car. I'll get it," I said, elbowing her out of the way.

"Don't be stupid," she snapped. "It'll be easier with two people." Before I could argue, she kneeled down and raised one side off the ground.

"Whatever," I said, exhaling heavily.

Even with the two of us, it took a bit of effort to carry the speaker inside and haul it down the narrow staircase to the storage cellar. Raina propped open the door with a crate, and we slowly dragged the speaker to a spot in the corner.

"Whew!" I exclaimed, sitting on top of it and running the back of my hand across my forehead.

Raina glanced around the cellar nervously. "Can we go now, Jase?"

"Just hold on a minute," I said. "I still need to go back and get Sylvester's tuner."

"I'll get it," she offered, then slipped out the door before I could protest. A few minutes later she came back and said, "Jase, the tuner isn't there."

"Of course it is. I usually store it in the glove box."

"Duh. I checked there first. It isn't anywhere in the van."

"But I know I brought it." I leaned against the bass rig and rubbed my forehead. "I had it when I tuned the Strat. Then I put it on top of the keyboards. . . ."

"Jase, it wasn't on the synthesizer when I loaded it. It must've fallen off when Roscoe was jumping around on that rickety stage."

I stood there dumbstruck for a moment, thinking back to the gig. She was right. One of those clunks and rattles I'd heard while Roscoe was doing his psycho bunny hop must have been the tuner tumbling behind the platform. Who knew if it was still there—if it had even survived the fall.

Searing anger flooded my circulatory system. "Damn!" I shouted, stamping my foot on the filthy floor. It was too much. First I'd gotten dumped and discarded in front of the entire town, then Raina had gotten all high-and-mighty on me, and then Sylvester's expensive tuner had ended up abandoned at a square-dance joint. What was next? Premature baldness? Hemorrhoids? My seventh-grade yearbook photo (before I discovered Clearasil) broadcast via satellite? What else could possibly go wrong?

"Damn!" I cried again, and kicked out at the nearest thing in my range.

The cellar echoed with a thunderous slam. It was then I realized that I'd kicked aside the apple crate Raina had used to prop open the door.

Twelve

"FACE IT, RAINA. We're stuck. Just give it up already." By then my rage was completely spent, replaced by a feeling of total, overwhelming defeat.

Raina tugged once again at the doorknob with all her might. "I can't believe this! This isn't happening!" she kept saying. "We've got to get out of here!"

"What does it matter?" I muttered. "If I go back out there, something awful will happen anyway. It's been like that for several days now. I should just stay in here, where nothing bad can reach me."

Raina stopped yanking on the knob long enough to glare at me. "Everything's always about you, isn't it? Poor Jason. The whole world is out to get you. Well, guess what! The world didn't cause this door to slam shut—*you* did!"

"It was an accident!" I shouted, leaping to my

feet. "I didn't do it on purpose! Just like I didn't force Trudy to ditch me or Roscoe to—"

"Stop it! I don't want to hear any more!" Raina clamped her hands over her ears and shook her head. "For three years you've gotten whatever you wanted, and now that you've suffered a small run of bad luck, you've fallen into the deepest pit of self-pity I've ever seen. This may come as a complete shock, but you are not the only individual on this planet with problems."

I turned my back to her and slouched against a speaker. I wasn't in the mood to debate Miss I'm-Always-Right. Arguing with Raina was about as pointless as trying to force that door open.

A familiar rattling sounded behind me. Raina was back at work, obviously with the notion that her efforts were worthwhile.

"Come on! Come on!" she yelled at the motionless slab of oak. "Oh, my God! I can feel something moving! It's working!"

Even though I was trying to ignore her, I couldn't help but glance in her direction. For a brief instant I wondered if tough little Raina could actually be dislodging the stuck door.

There was a loud clinking noise, and then Raina fell backward, the broken brass doorknob still in her grasp.

"Oh, no," she cried. "No, no, no, no, no!"

She looked so pitiful sitting there slumped over the door handle. Strands of hair veiled her face, and her hands seemed to tremble slightly. Something weird was up. Usually Raina acted as though she were tough enough to handle anything. It wasn't like her to break down this way.

As angry as I'd been at Raina, I couldn't stand to see her looking so pathetic. I was worried.

"Hey, Rain," I called softly. "It's all right. I mean, look at it this way: If a tornado hits the area, we're totally safe."

She didn't reply. Instead, she threw the severed knob across the room and doubled over in despair, grabbing her arms tightly in a sort of self-hug.

This was not good.

I walked over and put my hands on her shoulders. "Relax, Rain. We'll get out of here soon enough. I'm sure before long your parents will realize you aren't back yet and go searching for you."

"But they're out of town! They're visiting Aunt Hannah in Jacksonville!" Her voice was shaky and hysterical-sounding.

For the first time that night, I felt a pang of dread over our situation. I'd been counting on her family to send out a posse. My parents had gotten used to my arriving home late after a gig. They never waited up. Raina knew that too. Still, I didn't want to let my apprehension show, fearing it might make her panic even more.

"Don't worry. Someone will find us. Let's just kick back and play a game or something." I crouched down beside her. "What do you say? We can play Twenty Questions."

"No!" Raina stood up so fast she knocked me

back on my rear end. "We've got to get out of here! We just have to!"

She paced around the room like a madwoman, searching for something. I wasn't sure what she thought she'd find. Some explosives, maybe? A *Star Trek* phaser? A sign that read Secret Exit?

"There!" she exclaimed triumphantly, pointing to the top of the north wall. A tiny rectangle of a window—or a porthole, more precisely—cast a dim ray of moonlight onto the dusty floor.

"What? Are you nuts? You don't actually think we can escape through there, do you?"

"Well, maybe I could crawl through and go get help." She grabbed a couple of boxes and some apple crates and began stacking them underneath the window.

"Wait, Raina. Wait. Stop!" I grabbed her arm and took a case of pitted olives from her hands. "Think about this: Even if you made it up there without breaking your neck, you'd never fit through that opening. It's the size of a pet door."

She glanced about anxiously, her eyes large and wild-looking. "Then . . . then maybe we could yell for help until someone hears us and . . . and then they can let us out." She stood beneath the window, cupped her hands around her mouth, and screamed, "Hello! Hey! Is anyone out there?"

Raina continued to yell herself hoarse. For the first time I could remember, I was truly terrified—for her, rather than because of our predicament. I approached her cautiously and put my arms around her.

"Rain. Rain. Stop. Snap out of it," I said calmly but firmly. She struggled slightly, but I only tightened my grip. "No one can hear us down here. Just stop before you hurt yourself. Please?"

Suddenly, as if a switch had been thrown, Raina crumpled against me, sobbing. Her entire body was trembling, and I could actually feel the violent beat of her heart through her T-shirt. I walked her over to the wall opposite the window and set her down gently. As I took my seat beside her I continued to hold her around the shoulders, afraid that if I let go, she might shatter into pieces.

It hurt to see her this way, but I felt completely helpless to stop it. My other troubles suddenly seemed small and far away. Now all I wanted to do was protect her.

"What is it, Rain? What's wrong?" I asked her softly, brushing stray wisps of hair off her face. "You're scaring me. This isn't you."

Raina just leaned over and buried her face in my shoulder, still too choked up to speak. Finally, after a few minutes of thoroughly soaking my shirt, she sat up, took a deep, shuddery breath, and looked into my eyes helplessly. "I . . . I'm sort of claustrophobic," she whispered hoarsely.

"You're claustrophobic?" I repeated. *So that's why she's been losing it,* I thought. It seemed so weird that she'd never mentioned that to me before. I'd thought I knew everything about her.

She nodded weakly. "It's stupid, I know. For some reason, I've just always been really scared of closed-in places. Didn't you wonder why I hated coming down here—why I always asked you or someone else to come with me?"

"No," I mumbled, frowning. "I just thought it was because of, you know, the rats."

For a while Raina didn't say anything, but I could sense her tensing up even more. I wondered if my mentioning the rats might have made things worse.

"You know what?" I pulled her closer and rested the side of her head against the space below my collarbone. "You're okay. You're going to be okay."

Her body seemed to relax somewhat, but her quick, sharp breathing made me worry she might hyperventilate. Holding her firmly around the shoulders, I reached up and stroked her long, soft hair with my other hand. "Shh," I kept saying over and over again, which was strange, really, since she wasn't making a sound.

Outside, the crickets began their steady, rhythmic whirring, and a high-pitched whistle of wind sounded through the small panes of glass in the window. The night noises coupled with the earthy smell of the cellar made it almost seem like we were out in the open air.

That gave me an idea.

"Pretend we aren't here," I murmured into Raina's ear.

"How?" came her soft, muffled reply.

"Just tell yourself we're out camping near the

old fishing dock. Hear the bugs? The wind? The rustling of leaves?"

"Yes. But—"

"And can you smell the soggy swampland?"

She breathed in slowly. "Yes."

"Good. Now look over there," I said, gesturing. "What do you see?"

"A cement wall."

"No. That's Brushy Bayou off in the distance. You can see the stars reflecting in the water and the ripples made by the frogs. You and I have just finished dinner. Let's see . . . it was Mom's chicken salad sandwiches, a whole bag of jalapeño potato chips, and two ice-cold Cokes."

"Did you remember the Oreo cookies?" she asked.

I chuckled. "Yes. I brought them too, and we've eaten half the package already. Now we're just leaning back against the trees and skipping stones in the water." I pantomimed a tossing motion. "Mine hopped three times, yours hopped five. We throw some more. Mine hopped only twice. Yours hopped four times but, oops, you just ended up knocking a beaver senseless."

Quick gusts of air against my arm revealed her laughter. She seemed lighter now, less rigid and jittery. *Thank God,* I thought.

"So how do you feel?" I asked.

She paused briefly. Then, in a hushed, childlike voice, she replied, "Cold."

"Yeah, you forgot your jacket. I told you it

would get cold tonight on our camp-out, especially after the sun went down. But you never listen."

She snuggled in closer and looped her arms around my waist. It struck me how small and fragile she felt. I couldn't believe I'd been so mad at her. She was right—I'd been thinking only about myself lately. I'd been a jerk. And it *was* my fault that we were stuck down there. My fault that Raina was completely freaked out.

"Try to get some sleep," I said, rubbing her arms to keep her warm.

She tilted her head upward and met my eyes. "Will you sing me a song, Jase?" she asked faintly.

I smiled. "Sure."

I patted her elbow gently to keep time and launched into an a cappella version of "Jambalaya," followed by a couple of Creedence Clearwater Revival tunes. By the end of "Bad Moon Rising," her hands had loosened around my middle and her steady breathing let me know she was asleep. Just to make certain, I began a slower rendition of "Blue Eyes Crying in the Rain," but somewhere between the second and third verses, I drifted off.

I woke up sometime later, feeling totally disoriented. The overhead bulb had burned out at some point and the only light in the room came from the bluish moonbeams shining through the small window.

Raina was asleep with her head on my shoulder and her arms still wrapped around me. Her warm breath breezed gently against my neck, and her hair gave off the trademark floral scent that I'd grown so accustomed to. A shaft of moonlight was shining directly on her sleeping face, illuminating her features. She looked so beautiful, so delicate—almost like an angel. Without thinking, I reached up and gently stroked her cheek.

Raina's eyelids fluttered and opened. She gazed up at me, without saying a word, as my fingers slowly traced her eyebrows, nose, and mouth. Everything about her seemed so perfect, so soothingly familiar. Then all of a sudden, something pulled me toward her—or her toward me—until our mouths came together.

We kissed gently at first, my lips barely brushing over hers. Then it slowly deepened. Part of me couldn't believe I was kissing Raina, but a stronger part of me couldn't believe I'd never kissed her before. And soon I wasn't thinking at all. My mind was simply unusable, submerged in a swirling whirlpool of emotions. It all felt alive and electric and very, very *right*.

I don't know how long we kissed. It was as if everything else in the world ceased to exist. There was only us—Raina and me. Nothing else mattered.

Then, in a sudden movement, she pushed me away.

"Oh, my God!" she said, panic returning to her voice. "I can't believe I did that. I can't believe I *kissed* you."

Now I was the one who was panicking. I had just experienced the most mind-blowing, most *real* kiss ever, and here she was acting as though she had made the biggest mistake of her life. "What? Why?" I asked, reaching out for her again.

"Don't!" Her eyes were wide and frantic-looking. "Just don't!" She held her arm straight out in front of her, distancing me, and scooted farther down the wall.

"No," I said, scrambling over and grabbing her hands in mine. "Tell me why!"

"This is wrong," she said, wrenching free of my grasp.

"Wrong? How can you say that? How can you not feel how right this is?"

Raina shook her head vigorously. "This isn't about me. You're just mixed up about the whole Trudy thing."

Trudy? As my brain processed the name, I realized that I couldn't care less about her—in my mind, she was long forgotten. It seemed funny— for so long, I'd been obsessed with Trudy, but when it came down to it, she didn't mean anything to me. And Raina, who'd been nothing but a friend in my mind for so long, suddenly meant *everything*.

"No," I told her. "Trudy has nothing to do with this. I've been totally mixed up, I know. But now I see things clearly. Very clearly." I walked forward and placed my hands on her shoulders. "I know it's weird because we're best friends and everything, but don't you see—don't you feel—how much sense this makes?"

"Stop it!" she said, her voice quavering slightly. She twisted out from under my arms and turned away, covering her face with her hands. "Don't say that! You don't mean that!"

My mind reeled. Why was she acting this way? Why didn't she believe me? "I *do* mean it. More than anything," I said, stepping in front of her. "When we were kissing just now, it was . . . *incredible*. I know you felt it too, Raina. Don't tell me you didn't."

Raina lowered her hands and stared at me for a moment, her dark eyes growing soft and tender. Then she quickly looked away, and the anguish returned to her face. "What does it matter? To you it's just a game. You don't really care."

"How can you say that? What makes you so sure?" My voice was loud and edgy, but I couldn't help it.

"No. It would never work." She shook her head, biting her lip. Then she continued, in a quiet voice, "I would never put myself through that kind of pain."

I froze, letting her words slowly sink in. "Are you saying that you . . . don't trust me?"

She swallowed and looked down at the floor.

"Are you?" I repeated, my voice pleading.

But she never got to answer. Because right at that moment, the door burst open and two police officers raced into the room, their guns drawn.

Thirteen

"RAINA? RAIN, IT'S me. Open up," I called, knocking on the Baezes' front door for about the forty-third time.

I was desperate to continue our conversation from the night before. There's nothing like staring at the barrel of a shotgun to make you forget what you were talking about. Apparently someone had driven by the Scratchin' Post and had seen the van backed up to the rear door. Thinking a robbery was in progress, they called the cops. At first Officers Riley and Hernandez thought Raina and I were trying to steal all the equipment in the cellar. But after listening to our babbled explanations and making a late-night call to Sylvester, they let us go. Officer Hernandez took Raina home, so we hadn't been able to speak in private any longer.

After driving home exhausted, I ended up tossing and turning in my bed for the remaining few hours of night. I was so confused. Everything seemed different now, as if kissing Raina had somehow altered me. Either that or it had altered the rest of the world, making the things I'd thought I understood completely suddenly seem new and mysterious. Like Raina.

How could I have been so blind? For years the perfect girl had been right there beside me, and I'd never even known it. It was crazy. Just the day before, she'd been my buddy Raina, nagging at me about every little thing and shrugging off my remarks with that curl in her upper lip. Now when I thought about those lips, a tingling warmth spread over me, and I felt an overwhelming urge to join them with mine.

I had to find her and explain my feelings—as far as I could comprehend them myself. I knew she thought that I'd just been fooling around with her, that our kiss had been my way of passing time in the cellar. But how could she think that? Sure, I'd messed around with a lot of girls, but how could she not know that it was different with her?

We *had* to pursue this. It was too powerful to ignore. Only first I had to make her realize that I would never, ever hurt her.

I pounded on the door again, this time a little louder. "Rain, it's me. I need to talk to you."

Forty-four times and still no answer. The window curtains were shut tight and I couldn't hear the slightest noise from inside. Was she even there? I knew her parents had gone to Jacksonville, but I was sure Raina would be home at that hour. Maybe she was still asleep.

I walked around to her bedroom window and rapped on the screen. "Rain? Hey, Rainbow. It's Jase."

Nothing.

"Where is she?" I whispered to myself.

I drove home and tried calling her on the phone. Her answering machine picked up immediately.

"Give me a call, Rain," I said. "I have to see you."

It suddenly occurred to me that she might never have gone home. Maybe her parents were nervous about her staying there alone and arranged for her to sleep at a friend's house. I called up Casey, but she hadn't seen Raina since church on Sunday and suggested I try Renee. Renee told me in a groggy voice that Raina was definitely not there and that I should try Casey.

There was only one more person she might have stayed with. Raina wasn't exactly close friends with Shelly Armstrong, but her parents played bridge with Shelly's parents every weekend. It was possible they'd offered her a place to bunk.

"Hello?" came Shelly's southern drawl over the phone.

"Shelly, it's me. Jason."

There was a long pause. "Jason? Jason Lauderette?"

"Yeah. Uh, listen. I'm sorry to bother you, but by any chance is Raina staying over there?"

"No." Shelly sounded completely baffled. "Why do you ask?"

"It's just that . . . well . . . I can't find her, and I really need to talk to her."

"Are you guys in a fight?" she asked, a touch of glee in her voice.

"No. I mean, I don't think so. She just might not be talking to me."

"All right," she said flatly. "What did you do?"

"Me? Nothing! I didn't do a thing!" I protested.

"Yeah, right. You never do anything," she said sarcastically.

I sighed frustratedly. I should have known calling Shelly would be a big mistake. "Look, if you hear from Raina, could you just tell her we need to talk about something—something really important? Please?"

"Fine. But I'll do it for her, not you. I don't owe you anything."

Whatever, I thought irritably, and hung up the phone.

A photo of Raina from our first gig at the Scratchin' Post sat on my dresser. I picked it up and stared at it as if I were seeing it for the first time. The dainty curves of her mouth, which I had for so long associated with her fire-spitting sarcasm and friendly advice, now seemed like a soft invitation. Her piercing brown eyes now had a mesmerizing shimmer—as if they were lit up by moonbeams.

Where are you? I begged silently, outlining her face with my index finger.

Kissing Raina had been the most mind-opening thing that had ever happened to me. It had changed my life. I only hoped it hadn't driven away the best thing in it.

"Lookee here! If it isn't Jason Lauderette, professional cat burglar," Sylvester called with a laugh as I walked into the Post. "We were just talking about you, son." A couple of older locals sitting at the counter nodded at me and chuckled.

I managed to crack a polite smile, but just the slight reference to the previous night made my heart lurch. It was already early evening and still no word from Raina. By now my worry had ballooned to an obsessive panic that clamped around my stomach like an icy fist.

"Hey," I said to everyone. "Um, Sylvester, have you seen Raina?"

"Got a call this morning. Said she wasn't sure, but that she might not be in for her shift today. I told her that was understandable considering what y'all went through last night." He smiled broadly, his eyes twinkling as brightly as his gold tooth.

I held back the urge to punch that grin off his face. I was in no mood for kidding around. "Do you know where she was calling from?"

He shrugged. "Don't know."

"Do you think she'll be coming in?"

Again he lifted his shoulders. "Well, it's possible. But you know, her shift started half an hour ago."

"Just great," I mumbled, slouching onto a stool.

This had been my last chance to find Raina. All

day long I'd been either cruising around town in the van, checking out the likely places and looking for her car, or waiting in my room for the phone to ring. As each hour passed I grew more and more anxious, pacing the floor and mentally replaying scenes from the night before. I left a dozen messages on her machine. I checked my phone regularly to see if it had a dial tone. And I gazed at her picture constantly, as if it could give me the answers I needed.

"What's the matter, sonny?" Sylvester asked, leaning on the counter across from me. "You don't look like yourself."

"I don't feel like myself," I said in a low, hollow voice. It was true. I hadn't been this nervous and sweaty-palmed in years—it was as though I'd suddenly been transported back to junior high school.

Sylvester squinted at me. "What happened down there last night?"

"Nothing," I mumbled. "We just waited around and fell asleep." No way could I tell him what really happened—especially when I wasn't sure myself.

I checked my watch. It was six-thirty. Surely Raina had gotten my messages. Obviously she was avoiding me. But why? Why wouldn't she talk to me?

"Jason!" A female voice resounded through the café. I turned toward it, a twinge of hope quelling the conflict inside me. Raina! Finally!

My hopefulness immediately turned to shock. It was Trudy. Her eyes were wide, and a large smile had overtaken the lower half of her face.

"I was hoping I'd find you here!" she exclaimed, running toward me and waving a newspaper in one of her outstretched hands. "Look what I found!"

I just stared at her, speechless, trying to get a firm grip on reality. After all, the last time I'd seen Trudy, she had basically told me to get lost. But, strangely enough, I realized I didn't feel the least bit nervous around her. In fact, I felt nothing at all. It was as if everything I had gone through with her had happened to someone else entirely.

Trudy stood right beside me, her shoulder bumping mine, and spread out the paper on the counter. It was a copy of the *New Orleans Times-Picayune*.

"I bought this yesterday looking for Mother's wedding announcement, and guess what I saw!"

"What?" I asked, still eyeing her suspiciously. I half expected her to flash me a glacial stare and say, "your obituary" in an amused, haughty voice.

"See for yourself," she said, pointing to the top of the page.

I glanced down at the paper. Right underneath a headline that read "Around the State" was a lengthy article about Fourthfest, and tucked in the corner of printed text was a two-column-wide photo of our band. It was the promo shot I'd sent in with our demo tape, and a good one too. For one thing, you could actually see Martian behind the drums, and Roscoe looked very rock-and-roll in his polyester V-neck and baggies. I was slouched against a speaker trying to appear aloof and cool, and Raina . . . she looked beautiful. Her smile was framed by her two perfect dimples, and one shoulder was slightly cocked, as if she was feeling shy—or flirtatious.

Trudy's finger suddenly jabbed the page, blocking my view. "Read it!" she said excitedly. "This is a major newspaper. If it's listed here, it's the real thing!"

I scrutinized her face as she talked. I'd remembered Trudy as being flawlessly beautiful. But now I could see all sorts of imperfections in her. The tip of her nose tilted up at an abnormally sharp angle, her close-set eyes looked stony and severe, and her beauty-pageant smile didn't seem to illuminate any of her other features.

" . . . and it says Harry Connick Junior will be there. And that TV star—oh, what's his name? You know, the one on that family show?" She glanced over at me and caught me staring. "What? What are you looking at?"

"Nothing," I said coolly.

Trudy smiled and shook her head. "I know, I know. You're probably still mad at me about that whole Nelson thing. And I don't blame you."

She waited for a response, but I just sat there, eyeing her warily.

"The truth is," she continued, "I wanted to go out with *you*. It was just . . . well, you're *so* popular and all, and I couldn't handle all those girls fawning over you. I got jealous and then tried to get even by running off with Nelson."

Again she paused, but I remained silent. Did

she actually expect me to buy that? Did she think I was that desperate to have her back? Just one day earlier, hearing her say those things would have been music to my ears. Now it sounded phony and lame.

"It was stupid. My mistake entirely," she went on. "But what do you say we give it another try? Just start over?" She leaned in closer and raised her eyebrows expectantly.

My mind whirled. *She wants me? After everything that happened, she thinks we can actually go out?* I didn't know how I felt. Grateful? Happy? Angry? Nothing seemed to described the swirling vortex inside me. My thoughts just kept returning to Raina and the peaceful way she'd looked when she was sleeping in my arms.

But Raina didn't want me. That was becoming more and more clear. If she did, she would have contacted me already. Obviously she didn't take my feelings seriously. *Or maybe*—my gut seized as I turned over a new, more frightening thought— *she doesn't feel the same way about me as I do about her!*

"So how about it?" Trudy murmured, running her hand along my arm. "I know I totally screwed things up, but I promise I'll make it up to you."

I looked into Trudy's face—at her sly grin, her smug, calculating expression. Strangely, I could see myself the way I'd been just days before, and the careless way I'd treated girls in the past. A flash of hatred passed through me.

"So . . . what's your number again?" I asked, forcing a smile.

Trudy's eyes flickered triumphantly. She dug a pen out of her purse and scribbled down seven digits on a paper napkin.

"Great," I said, folding the napkin and placing it in my shirt pocket. "Maybe I'll give you a call sometime."

For a brief instant an insulted look crossed Trudy's face. Then it quickly vanished.

"Yeah, you keep that handy," she said. "I think you'll find you'll need it." Before I realized what was happening, she threw her arms around my neck and gave me a long, defiant kiss.

I sat there, rigid as a statue, as she locked her lips on mine. It seemed strange that I had once dreamed about Trudy's kissing me. I'd imagined it would be fiery and electric, but now I just felt numb. It was nothing at all like the earthshaking kiss with Raina.

Trudy pulled away and flashed me a wicked grin. "Until later," she said in a low, sultry voice. Then she turned and walked back through the dining room toward the exit.

As my eyes followed her, they caught sight of a familiar figure standing motionless by the bar.

Raina.

Her mouth was open slightly, and her eyes flickered with emotion. She looked as though she was about to cry.

My heart twisted. "Raina!" I shouted, jumping up. She shook her head and started backing away.

Tears began streaming down her cheeks.

"Raina, stop! I need to talk to you!"

Before I could take another step, she turned and ran out of the restaurant. I saw a streak of blond hair, and then she was gone. A slight scent of flowers hung in the air, the only evidence of her having been there—unless you count the image of her tearstained face, which had been burned into my mind.

I stood in the middle of the dining room, paralyzed. The dining room dissolved, and I was back in the cellar the night before, crouched beside Raina in the darkness. "Are you saying you don't trust me?" I was asking her.

Her stricken face a moment before had told me my worst fears were confirmed. She thought I was using her. And now she probably assumed I'd gone back to Trudy.

I'd really blown it this time. I'd lost the most important person in my life.

Possibly forever.

Fourteen

FOR THE SECOND time in eight hours I drove all over town looking for Raina. But it was no use. At least one fact managed to penetrate my hard head that day: *If Raina doesn't want you to find her, you can't.*

Eventually I returned home and went up to my room to sulk. My body felt both weary and restless, and my mind was simultaneously muddled and pre-occupied. I'd heard about people who travel overseas so much they forget where they are and what day it is. That was me.

I flopped down on my bed and covered my head with my pillow, as if it could somehow muffle the pain inside. *Why'd you let Trudy kiss you?* I thought miserably. *Now Raina will never believe you're serious about her.*

As awful as the experience had been, one good thing had come from the situation. I now had no doubt that Raina had feelings for me. Or at least she used to. Just thinking about that hurt look on her face made me hate myself even more.

Suddenly a rapping sound took me out of my thoughts.

"What?" I barked out, my head resurfacing from under the pillow. I figured it was Mom coming to tell me dinner was ready, and hunger was the one physical sensation my body wasn't experiencing.

The door opened, and there stood Raina.

"Rain!" I exclaimed, jumping off the bed. I led her into the room and shut the door. "Thank God! I've been going nuts trying to find you. We've got to talk."

Raina gazed at me blankly. Her tears were gone, and her face was devoid of any emotion whatsoever. "I can't stay," she said quickly.

"Aw, come on. Let's just sit down for a while and—"

"I only came because I thought it was fair to tell you this now, while there was still time for you to make other plans."

I frowned, puzzled. "Tell me what?"

"That I'm quitting the band."

"What? But you can't!" I paused, softening my pitch. "Does this have something to do with what happened in the cellar?"

Raina just stood there, staring mutely at the floor.

"I don't understand, Rain. Why won't you talk about this? Why wouldn't you return my calls?"

My voice took on a desperate edge, but I couldn't help it.

"Because I needed to get my head straight," she said finally. "Because I wasn't sure if I was ready . . . to tell you how I feel."

"How do you feel?" I asked gently.

She paused, looking back down at the rug. "I'm still not ready to say."

"But why?"

"Because I'm scared!" she yelled, a sob cutting through her words.

"Of me?" I placed my arms around her. "Raina, you don't need to worry about—"

"Yes, I do!" she screamed, ducking away from me and walking over to the window. "I know you too well, Jase. I've seen what you can do. And I was afraid if I let my guard down with you, I'd just end up getting played." She turned and faced me, her dark eyes hardening. "Which is obviously what's happening."

"No! No, it's not," I protested. "Look, what you saw with me and Trudy—that was nothing. *She* kissed me! I swear! She means nothing to me anymore."

Raina held up a hand. "Save it, Jase. You forget who you're sweet-talking. I've heard you smooth your way out of sticky situations for years, and I know all your tricks."

"But it's not like that," I pleaded, shaking my head. "This is different. *I'm* different. You've got to hear me out."

"I've got to go," she said wearily. She brushed past me and grabbed the door handle.

"Wait." I reached out and grasped her arm. "Please, Rain, can't we work this out? For us. For the sake of . . ." I paused, reaching for the right word—anything to make her stay. "For the sake of our *friendship?*"

Her eyes clouded over. "No," she replied, her voice barely a whisper. "Because I can't be your friend."

Then she threw open the door and raced out of the room.

I collapsed onto my bed, feeling heavy with despair. What had I done? I'd ruined everything. Now not only was Raina giving up on her feelings for me, she was giving up on our friendship—and the band.

But I couldn't blame her for not trusting me. It was completely my fault—she'd tried to warn me all along. My hooking up with tons of girls over the past couple of years had come back to haunt me. And suddenly I could see how horrible I'd been to those girls. I'd been worse than Trudy—right up there with convicted felons and flesh-eating bacteria.

And I didn't deserve Raina.

I didn't feel like doing anything. I didn't think that I'd ever feel like doing anything ever again. So I lay down in bed. Then, while staring at Raina's photo on my dresser, I let the tears flow.

*　　*　　*

I woke up in the middle of the night, exactly seven hours after Raina had run out on me. Sleep hadn't cleared my mind any. I was still so miserable, I couldn't comprehend my own thoughts. And I knew that for the first time ever, I couldn't talk out my problems with Raina. That made it worse.

"Face it, Lauderette. You're too lame to live," I mumbled. I rolled over and threw a blanket over my head with my right hand, letting my left hand fall to the floor.

Spronggg! My fingers scraped against my acoustic guitar, which was stashed beneath my bed.

I ran my hand along the familiar curve of the guitar's body and the springy, elastic tension of the strings. At least *it* was the same as I'd remembered. I suddenly thought of Sylvester and how he'd always encouraged me to open up to my guitar, as if it were a close friend. "Playing can help unburden your soul," he'd say, "and sometimes a little of your soul ends up in the music."

I sat up and picked my Yamaha off the floor. Then I carefully dusted it off and tuned it. I hadn't played it in a while. In fact, I hadn't picked it up since the Trudy/Nelson fiasco. We had lots to talk about.

At first I strummed a few chords and picked out a scale or two. Then I let the music emerge on its own. A barrage of sounds emanated from the instrument. Harsh, discordant riffs. Drawn-out wailing notes. I could almost feel my emotions channeling through my fingers.

As I played, I kept thinking about how Raina had stormed out of my room. The hatred in her voice. The pain in her eyes. I recalled all the moments we had sat there, laughing about the band or talking about our lives. And I thought about the times she'd tried to warn me about my attitude with girls, teasing me about getting in trouble someday.

Eventually my mind traveled back to the night in the cellar.

Closing my eyes, I could almost feel her in my arms and picture her serene, sleeping face against my shoulder. I could even smell her sweet floral scent mixing with the odor of grime and mildew. And I remembered our kiss.

Out of nowhere, a melody welled up in my head. But instead of capturing my bitter despair, the tune was lilting and hopeful: a soft ballad. Lyrics came to me—about friendship catching fire, a devotion deepening. Before long, we'd composed an entire song, my guitar and I, and it was as if my music were trying to tell me something. Something I hadn't put into words until then.

I was in love with Raina. Real, unmistakable love.

Why I hadn't admitted it before was a complete mystery. I'd known since I kissed Raina that she was the one for me—always had been. But it took my music to reveal the total truth.

I should have told her. Here I'd been so hung up on getting her to admit her feelings, and I wouldn't even admit mine.

The final chord rang out and slowly dissipated. I carefully set down the guitar and ran my hand along its strings. I felt as though I'd bonded with it. It had certainly been a friend when I needed one the most.

"It's just you and me now," I said sadly. "And a heck of a good song."

The next morning I woke up energized. I don't know if I felt inspired by my late-night musical breakthrough or what, but all of a sudden I knew exactly what I needed to do. I needed to make things right.

As soon as I was dressed, I jumped in my van, drove six blocks over, and knocked on a door. A few seconds later Shelly Armstrong greeted me with a bewildered expression.

I took a deep breath and began to speak. "Hi. I'm sorry to bother you so early like this. I just came over to say I was sorry. You were right. I treated you like dirt. You deserve someone better—someone who'll treat you with real respect. Anyway, I just wanted you to know that if I could take it all back, I would. Well . . . I really should go now. I'll see you at Fourthfest, I hope. Bye."

Then I gave a final wave and walked off, leaving Shelly frozen in her doorway, her mouth as wide as a cereal bowl.

One down, several more to go, I thought. *Then maybe I'll be a little closer to deserving Raina.*

Roscoe grabbed his bass as if he were choking it and ripped off a loud, inharmonious chord. The walls of the garage seemed to shudder.

"Man, this stinks!" he groaned.

My thoughts exactly.

It was later that evening, and our final rehearsal before Fourthfest had taken on the mood of a funeral.

"It's because of Raina, you know," came Martian's voice from behind the wall of drums. "It just doesn't sound right without her."

"It doesn't feel right either," I mumbled, taking off my guitar. I slumped down next to the speaker and stared at Raina's abandoned keyboard. Just the sight of it filled me with guilt.

So much for good intentions. After a long day of apologizing to ex-girlfriends, I'd felt a little better about facing Raina, so I'd driven over to the Scratchin' Post, determined to win her back. I told her I needed to speak with her in private, that I'd done a lot of soul-searching and figured out my feelings. But she'd just kept busing tables and refilling people's iced-tea glasses, totally ignoring me. Finally Sylvester came over and asked me to leave her alone. I had no idea how much he understood of the situation, but he patted my shoulder reassuringly and said, "Give it some time, son. She'll come around."

Time? How much time? I wondered. *The band needs her now. I need her.*

"You know, for someone who got on my back

all the time, I'm sure gonna miss her," Roscoe muttered, setting his bass onto its stand.

"Can't you talk to her, Jason?" Martian whined. "Can't you make her change her mind?"

I shrugged. There was nothing I wanted to do more, but I was totally out of ideas. If only I could somehow *prove* my feelings for her, produce some evidence to back up my words, then maybe she'd realize I'd changed.

"I don't understand why she had to quit anyway," Martian grumbled, trudging out from behind his drums. "It was, like, out of nowhere. Especially when we're finally getting real exposure."

"Was it because of the Monroe gig?" Roscoe asked, worried.

"No, it had nothing to do with that," I replied with a sigh. "It's me she has a problem with."

The guys exchanged suspicious glances.

"What did you do?" Martian asked.

"I know." Roscoe pointed a bony finger at me. "Did she finally get tired of all your women?"

"No," I responded, rolling my eyes. "And there's not going to be any more of that either." I walked over to the deck railing and looked out over the bayou. "I'm through messing around with girls."

I announced this last part calmly, matter-of-factly—as if I were commenting on the weather. The thing was, I didn't feel any remorse at all. I simply had no desire to go out with a girl I wasn't crazy about.

"You what?" Roscoe burst out laughing. "Yeah, right. Good one, Lauderette."

I turned around so they could see my expression. "I mean it," I said. "From now on, there's just one girl I want."

"Don't tell me you're still flipped out over Trudy!" Martian gasped. "Even after what she did?"

"No, it's not Trudy," I said, shaking my head. Then I sucked in my breath and looked right into their faces, my heart suddenly accelerating. "It's Raina," I blurted out. "I love Raina."

Roscoe and Martian exchanged glances again. I half expected them to fall down giggling, but instead they stepped off the stage and strolled over to me, clapping me on the back.

"Dude, we thought you'd never see the light," Roscoe said, grinning.

"Yeah," Martian echoed. "If you didn't wise up soon, we were gonna lock you in the cellar . . . again."

My jaw unhinged. "You mean . . . you *knew*?" How could they have known about it? Especially when I hadn't realized it myself until recently.

"Man, how could we not?" Roscoe replied. "You guys bicker as much as an old married couple, and you've been inseparable for years."

"But . . . but I went out with all those other girls," I went on. "Didn't you wonder about that?"

Martian chuckled. "Aw, come on. Didn't you wonder why you only stayed with those girls a week or two? They were so wrong for you. They weren't *her*."

I nodded slowly, my head spinning. So Roscoe and Martian had figured out my love life before I had. How lame did that make me?

"You know, Jase, you still haven't explained what all this has to do with Raina quitting," Roscoe said, lowering his voice.

A heavy sigh deflated me, slumping me back against the railing. "Guys, I really screwed up," I mumbled. Then I told them the entire ordeal— from Raina and me kissing in the cellar, to Trudy coming on to me in the café, to my eventual conversion into a decent person. It felt good to finally unload it all. And by the time I'd finished, a large amount of frustration had worked its way out of me.

"So what are you going to do now?" Roscoe asked.

"Yeah," Martian chimed in. "You have to get her back."

Their support made me feel stronger—more capable. I smiled. And in the recesses of my troubled mind, a plan started to form. "You know, Raina said she wasn't going to Fourthfest, not even to watch. But we have to get her there somehow." I rubbed my chin thoughtfully. "I have an idea how to make that happen, but it'll take all of us working together. You guys in?"

"Hey, we're a band, aren't we?" Martian said.

Roscoe gave me a high five. "Just say the word, man."

"Thanks, guys. I'll tell you what we need to do. But first"—I pointed to our deserted instruments— "I have a new song for us to learn."

Fifteen

IT WAS FOURTHFEST, and the biggest day of my life. This would be my chance to prove myself as a musician. And, more important, this would be my chance to prove my feelings to Raina.

There were still three hours to kill before our set, and I was too restless to wait in the old, un-air-conditioned school bus the managers had provided as a dressing room. I walked away from Martian and Roscoe, who were waiting for Harry Connick Jr.'s bus to pull in, and headed out to the main grounds.

I balked when I saw the swarms of people. It looked as if the populations of six parishes had converged on the farm. But I shouldn't have been surprised. Fourthfest was by far the coolest event in that part of the country. Imagine a huge outdoor barbecue with all of your friends and several of your favorite bands providing music—that's what it was like. And that year, instead of standing on the grass with a group of my buddies, I'd be the one pleasing the crowd (or at least trying to) on the stage. I was so nervous and excited, I could barely walk and breathe at the same time.

I wandered through the crowds, taking in the range of sensations the festival had to offer. Everything was in full swing. Red, white, and blue flags colored the landscape. The odors of homemade jambalaya, étouffée, red beans and rice, and deep-fried turkeys wafted from the food booths. And the ground throbbed with the rhythm of an awesome zydeco band onstage.

Everywhere I went, people came up to greet me. Brenda was there, working a face-painting tent along with the other dance squad members. I passed Kimmy and Junie in line for sodas. Tony Brewer waved a turkey leg at me as he sat on a hay bale talking with his buddies. At one point Casey and Renee ran up to tell me that John Goodman was supposedly somewhere in the crowd, then they quickly disappeared into the sea of people. Even Shelly told me to "break a leg"—and I was pretty sure she meant it in a good way.

"Hello, Jason," someone else called out.

I turned around to see Trudy sauntering up to me, wearing a wide, phony grin. She was still beautiful, but I could barely stand the sight of her.

"I thought you were going to call," she said, raising her eyebrows.

I shrugged. "Sorry. I had other things to do."

"Mmm-hmmm. So . . . this is Fourthfest," she said, glancing around.

"Yes," I replied impatiently. I really, really didn't want to talk to her. My mind was already crammed too full to deal with whatever she had up her sleeve.

All of a sudden squeals welled up from the crowd and a wave of people ran over to the back gate. Dressed in a Hawaiian shirt, big floppy hat, and cutoffs, Kurt Loder shuffled into the grounds, followed by an MTV film crew.

Trudy nudged my shoulder to regain my attention. "So, did you come here alone?"

I could feel my face cloud over as my thoughts returned to Raina. Yes. I was definitely alone.

Trudy read my expression and pounced like a cat. "That's too bad," she crooned, sliding a hand up my arm. "You know, I could keep you company until your set. How about you show me around backstage? Then maybe later we could take in some . . . fireworks?"

My back went rigid. Trudy was the *last* person I wanted to spend the day with. I stared at her, wondering how I'd ever fallen for someone like that—someone so shallow and self-absorbed. *Just like I used to be,* I thought, silently cursing myself.

"I don't think so, Trudy," I told her, gently removing her hand.

For a quick moment she couldn't hide her shock. Then she laughed awkwardly. "Oh, come on. This is such a big deal. Wouldn't it be more fun to share it with someone?"

"That's exactly what I plan to do," I remarked. "Only not with you."

Trudy's smile vanished. Her eyes frosted over.

"Good-bye, Trudy. I hope you enjoy the show," I called out as I walked away, heading toward the backstage gate.

As I reached the rear yard, I breathed a huge sigh of relief. Turning down Trudy made me feel lighter, freer somehow. It suddenly occurred to me that I'd never refused a pretty girl before. But then, this day was all about saying good-bye to my old self and starting anew.

After all, they don't call it Independence Day for nothing.

"Where's Martian?" I asked Roscoe as I mounted the steps of the school bus.

"Putting our plan into action," he sang out.

"Good." I plopped down on a green vinyl seat, suddenly feeling nervous again. It wouldn't be long now. In a matter of hours I'd be singing in front of the entire Fourthfest crowd. And Raina too, if everything worked out. *She has to come,* I thought, anxiously bouncing my leg up and down. *The show will mean nothing without her here.*

"I got to meet Harry!" Roscoe told me.

"That's nice."

"And Kurt Loder too. Man, that dude's a spaz!"

"Mmm-hmmm. Great."

Roscoe leaned forward and drummed on the back of the seat in front of him. "Kurt says he's gonna interview us after our set. And he totally dug my fake tuxedo shirt. What'd I tell you guys? Wear the right duds and the media come calling!"

"Yeah," I said, barely hearing whatever Roscoe was saying.

"Come on, dude." Roscoe reached over and tapped his bony knuckles against my shoulder. "Buck up. Raina will come. I just know it."

I stared back at him. "You think so?"

"The forces are in motion. You just wait."

I nodded, letting out a deep breath. It had to work—it just had to. I mean, the past couple of days had given me a glimpse of what life would be like without Raina. In a word: purgatory. I'd never felt so completely alone and undone. It was as if I weren't completely whole without her.

"Jason! I'm back!" Martian's voice broke through my thoughts.

As soon as he came into view, a steady torrent of questions flowed from my mouth. "Did you make the call? Is she coming? What'd she say? How did she sound?"

"Whoa, whoa," Roscoe said. "Let the little dude talk."

Martian glared at Roscoe and then turned to me. "Just like you told me to, I called her and told her we'd accidentally left the guitar amp in your garage. I said your parents weren't home and asked if she would please bring it over. She yelled at me a little while, but finally she said she'd do it."

"Yes!" I cheered, jumping up. "Martian, you're

my hero!" My heart lifted. I hadn't felt this hopeful in days.

"So what do we do now?" Martian asked.

"We wait," I replied, rubbing my hands together. "We wait and we hope and we pray."

His face fell. "Oh. I was hoping we could visit Harry Connick Junior before our set started."

Less than ten minutes to go and she still hadn't arrived. I was going stark raving mad. Everything depended on this plan. Raina had to be there—it was my only chance to prove my feelings to her. Besides, we couldn't perform without the amp anyway.

"Where is she, man?" Roscoe asked, bouncing in his high-top sneakers. "We don't have any more time."

Roscoe, Martian, and I stood offstage behind the large chain-link fence that separated the performers from the audience. I could tell my bandmates were as nervous as I was. Roscoe tapped out a rhythm against the fence post that was twice as fast as the song Paul Minor and His Orchestra was performing. And Martian just kept staring at his watch and saying, "Whoa."

"Relax, guys," I said, trying to mask the shakiness in my voice. "We still have a few minutes. Just kick back and jam to the music."

Yeah, right, I thought. *Like that's possible.* The last couple of hours had passed like years, and I hadn't been able to enjoy the show at all.

What's taking her so long? I wondered. *Did she change her mind?*

No. There was no way. Even though she was upset with me, it wouldn't be like her to let down the band. She'd be there. Something inside me couldn't give up hope just yet.

A few minutes later Paul Minor thanked the audience and announced his last song. I scanned the back road for Raina's car. Still nothing. Panic wrenched my stomach, and I could feel my nerves fraying like worn shoelaces.

"Whoa," Martian moaned, following my gaze.

"Just chill. We're not sunk yet," I said, trying to reassure myself more than him. But a nagging doubt was beginning to take hold of me. She should have arrived already. Could she have been hurt in a car accident? Or did she simply detest me too much to do us the favor? Either explanation was horrible.

"Yo, Jason!" I glanced up and saw Sylvester grinning through the fence.

"Hey! What are you doing here?" I asked him, taken aback. I'd never seen Sylvester at a Fourthfest. He'd always said he was too old to stand in the sun all day.

He gestured to the crowd around him. "Same as everyone else. I closed down the café, since most folks were out here, but I'm making a mighty nice profit at my gumbo booth," he said, chuckling. "Looks like you're going to have yourself a big day too."

A pang of anxiety sliced through me. "I don't know," I mumbled. "I hope so."

Sylvester pointed a callused finger through one of the chain-link diamonds, tapping me on the chest. "You got to have faith, boy," he urged. "Faith in yourself—and the people around you. That's how you make your dreams happen."

I forced a smile. If he only knew I was about to take the stage without a guitar amp and without the girl of my dreams by my side, he probably wouldn't be so encouraging. Still, Sylvester had always been a sort of hero of mine, and it meant a lot to see him there. *At least* he *came,* I thought glumly.

Suddenly applause thundered around us. The emcee came onstage and thanked Paul Minor for his set. Then he announced that after a short break, the Bankheads would be performing. Another cheer welled up from the crowd.

"Well, that's your cue," Sylvester remarked, stepping away from the fence. "Break a leg, son. We're all rooting for you."

"Thanks," I replied, watching him stroll away. Then I turned back toward Roscoe and Martian, who looked near death with panic.

"Whoa! What are we going to do?" Martian cried, tugging at my arm. "It's time for us to set up!"

I glanced over at the stage and swallowed hard. "Raina's still not here yet?" I asked, hoping beyond hope.

"No," Roscoe replied, his face pale. "Man,

we're toast. No amp, no gig. No gig, no MTV interview. No MTV interview—"

"All right! All right!" I hollered. "I get your point."

"What do we do? What do we do? What do we do?" Martian cracked his knuckles and hopped up and down nervously.

I took one last look down the rear gravel drive, pleading with every ounce of my being for Raina to appear. But the road remained vacant and forbidding—not even a mosquito crossed its path.

Face it, Lauderette, I told myself. *It's over. She's not coming.* The realization coursed through me like liquid cement, slowly weighing me down. Her absence could mean only one thing: She hated me. Raina would never have thwarted our big break like this unless she totally and truly despised me.

My knees almost buckled, and I had to reach up and grab the fence for support. Some great plan. Now everything was ruined. First I'd let down Raina, and now I'd let down the band. I was totally unworthy as a human being—a vile, loathsome waste of cells.

"Come on, man! Snap out of it!" Roscoe shook me by the shoulders. "We need you!"

I blinked up at him in a daze. Then I turned and stared into Martian's panic-stricken face. *They need me?* I wondered. *How can they need me? What can I possibly do?*

Suddenly Sylvester's words echoed through my head. *You've got to have faith.*

He was right. Raina had had faith in me. She had pushed me toward my dream of making it as a musician, and now here I was, about to play at Fourthfest. I might have lost Raina, but I still had the chance to reach my goal.

I had to go for it. For the guys. For me. And for the me Raina had once believed in.

"Well? Why are you guys just standing there?" I asked, determination returning to my voice. "You need to go set up. In the meantime, I'm going to see if I can borrow an amp from one of the other bands."

Roscoe and Martian traded puzzled glances, then turned and headed for their equipment. Paul Minor and His Orchestra had just cleared the stage. While the other guys hooked up their instruments, I approached Minor and told him about our predicament. He was really cool about it and said he'd lend me his amp, no problem.

"It's right down there, by our truck," he said, pointing to a blue Suburban parked by the road. "You're welcome to it."

"Thanks," I called out as I took off running. "You're a lifesaver."

As I raced for the amp, dodging equipment and stagehands, I felt curiously empty inside. The nervousness was still there—which was understandable, since I was about to play in front of thousands of people—but every other sensation was gone. It was as if knowing that Raina was out of my life made everything else less meaningful. Even if I did manage to fulfill my dream of becoming a successful musician, would it matter as much without her to share it with?

But I couldn't waste time thinking about that now. I had to focus on our set and shove all other thoughts aside. That was the only way to get through this.

I reached the truck and was bending down to pick up the amp when I noticed a cloud of dust billowing down the back road. It was a car.

My heart started to beat double-time. It was Raina's Honda!

She came!

I watched, dumbstruck with happiness, as Raina's car came toward me, eventually skidding to a stop right in back of the stage platform.

"I'm sorry!" she cried, leaping out and popping open the back hatch. "Your neighbor, Mrs. Sapp, caught me sneaking into your garage and threatened to call the cops. It took forever to explain it all. Then traffic was a total nightmare because everyone was heading out here. I probably could've walked faster." Her voice strained as she yanked at the heavy guitar rig.

"Hey, hey, I've got that," I told her, practically bouncing up to the car. I was so glad to see her, I could have launched myself into space. "Thanks so much for bringing this, Rain."

She jumped slightly, as if startled to have me so near. "You're welcome," she said, the frantic pitch disappearing from her voice.

Her eyes drooped as she met my gaze, and tiny creases erupted on her forehead. She looked so small and fragile—all I wanted to do was reach out and hold her.

I lifted the amp from her car and gently set it on the ground. "Listen," I began, trying to sound calm and casual, "why don't you stick around awhile and watch our set?" I held my breath as I studied her reaction.

She cocked one shoulder and stared down at the gravel beneath her feet. "I don't know," she replied softly.

A desperate chill came over me. I *had* to make her stay. "Please, Raina," I pleaded, grabbing her hands in mine. "You're a part of this too. Or at least you were."

She exhaled slowly, gazing at our clasped hands. My pulse throbbed faster than one of Martian's drum solos.

"Okay," she said finally, the corners of her mouth rising slightly.

"Great!" I cheered. "We're on in, like, two minutes. I should probably get back." I hesitated briefly, fearful that she'd disappear the minute I turned away.

"Jase, I'm only staying for your show because the music means a lot to me," Raina said. "But that's it. After that I'm heading back." She pursed her lips and folded her arms across her chest.

"Okay." I nodded. "That's all I ask."

I took one last look at her and then wrenched

my eyes away, heading toward the stage. The murmur of thousands of spectators grew louder as I neared the bandstand, but I barely paid attention. No matter how many people were there, I knew I'd be playing for only one.

As quickly as I could I heaved the amp up the backstage steps and rolled it onstage. The other guys had already finished setting up. Roscoe gave me a hurry-up signal as he strapped on his bass. A stagehand provided me with a mike, and I plugged in my guitar, checking the tuning. Soon everything was ready.

The emcee nodded at us and took the stage. "Ladies and gentlemen, please give a warm welcome to . . . the Bankheads!"

The ocean of spectators before me clapped and cheered. For a second I was overcome. It was my moment. Then I caught a glimpse of Raina standing at the side of the stage. *Correction,* I thought. *This is* our *moment.*

"Thanks. Happy Fourth of July!" I called to the crowd. "I'd like to start with a brand-new song, for someone very important to me."

I tapped the mike and cleared my throat. Then, looking over at Raina, I hit the first chord and started singing.

Raina
You hold me up when you hold my hand
You keep me whole when you
keep my secrets inside

I don't have to hide
When I'm with you

Raina
You make me laugh, you make me better
You reached in to pull me out of this hole
that I call my soul
And you saved me

I found a song I'd never heard
With just my guitar to confide in
It's your music, it's your words
That was always playing inside me

Throughout the entire song, I kept my gaze fixed on Raina. Her eyes seemed to grow wider with every note, and her lips parted in silent amazement. The rest of the world was forgotten. There was only me, Raina, and the music.

I shut my eyes as I belted out the closing line, letting the last note hang in the air. Then the music tapered off on a final, happy note. A loud rumble welled up from the crowd.

"Now *that's* a song!" Sylvester hollered from the front row.

Instead of bowing to the fans, I placed my guitar on the stand and walked over to Raina, pulling her onto the stage.

"What are you doing?" she asked. Tears were streaming down her face, but she was smiling—her warm, open, signature smile. Man, I'd missed that smile.

The applause grew louder as we reemerged from the wings. But I was only vaguely aware of the audience, the TV cameras, even the rest of the band. All I knew was that I needed her beside me.

Roscoe, always the media monger, held a live mike underneath me as I spoke. But I didn't care.

"You made this happen," I said to Raina, my voice echoing out over the grounds. "You're a part of this—a part of me. I love you, Raina."

Her dark eyes glittered like fireworks and her lips trembled slightly as she said, "I love you too."

Cupping her face in my hands, I leaned forward and kissed her tenderly. The crowd went wild. Cameras rolled. Roscoe barked out a cheer into the mike. And I got lost in the intensity of the kiss.

After a wonderful, immeasurable moment, we pulled back, smiling secretly at each other.

"You know," I whispered, "we forgot the amp, but we *did* remember to pack up your keyboard and bring it with us. Feel like helping out your old band?"

She laughed. "Why not? I wouldn't want to do anything to prevent your big dream from coming true."

"Oh, don't worry about that," I murmured, my lips closing in on hers. "It already has."

ARE YOU A PLAYER?

You know that old stereotype that says all guys are total users and all girls are always looking for serious, committed relationships? Guess what—plenty of guys are true-blue, and plenty of *girls* are anything but! Do you know which category you fit into? Take Jenny and Jake's love quiz to find out if you're a major-league *player*.

1. *You and your date go to see the latest horror movie. Your eyes are glued to:*

A. The screen, while you reach out to grab your date's hand—and squeeze hard!

B. Your guy's profile—what else could be worth looking at?

C. The gorgeous blond guy a few rows away— you're thinking of a way to separate from your date after the movie just long enough to snag the other guy's phone number.

2. *The last time you canceled a date with your boyfriend was:*

A. *Cancel time with my boyfriend? What are you thinking?*

B. Last weekend, when the guy down the street asked me out at the last minute.

C. The time my best friend found out her parents were getting divorced, and I knew she needed my support big-time.

3. *Your boyfriend invites you to hang with him and his buddies. Your first thought:*

A. Yes! This must mean he really cares about me and wants me to be a part of his life.

B. No! I can't share a single second of our time together with anyone else.

C. Yes! It's a chance to get to know those delicious-looking friends of his.

4. *You use the words "I love you":*

A. When you want something from a guy, or when you're trying to reassure him that he really is more special to you than Mike, Raphael, Reuben, Frank . . .

B. In every other sentence you say to your snookie-wookums.

C. Only when you're sure that you truly mean them, and only with that one special guy in your life.

5. *Under what circumstances would you lie to your boyfriend?*

A. None. Honesty and trust are the fundamental elements of a healthy relationship.

B. If he actually expects me to tell him where I *really* was last night.

C. Well, there was the time I pretended my whole family left the city for Christmas in order to get him to invite me to spend the holiday with him. After all, I couldn't bear the thought of one day apart!

6. *You're newly single, and three adorable guys ask you out for the same night. You:*

A. Turn them all down—you need time to figure out how to win back your ex, since you're convinced that his move to the other side of the globe and his new girlfriend are only minor obstacles to your undying love for each other.

B. Agree to all three dates—scheduling one after the other so there's time to squeeze them all in!

C. Agree to go out with the guy with whom you have the most relationship potential, and tell the other two you'd like to stay friends.

7. *Cheating on a boyfriend is:*

A. Only a problem if you get caught.

B. Any romantic or physical involvement with another guy.

C. Everything from thinking a guy on TV looks cute to having a conversation with another member of the opposite sex.

8. *Your boyfriend asks you—in that pseudocasual but obviously curious tone—how many guys you've kissed. Your response:*

A. You quickly throw out a single-digit number before reassuring him that he is (of course) the best of them all.

B. You explain with an apologetic smile that you actually can't count that high.

C. You swear that his mouth is the only one your lips have touched, and that it will be until the day you die.

9. *When you break up with a guy, things between you two afterward are usually:*

A. On friendly terms. We move on, but we don't hate each other.

B. Extraordinarily, unbearably painful. I cannot survive without the love of my life.

C. Pretty bitter. For some reason, they seem to get awfully angry about the fact that I wasn't exactly *completely* monogamous.

10. *When you picture your dream man, he is:*

A. Absolutely perfect. The only guy who could satisfy me would have to be utterly flawless, down to his neatly groomed cuticles.

B. Sensitive and gentle, with a great sense of humor and a warm heart. Okay, maybe he has beautiful eyes and a decent smile too.

C. My boyfriend—he's my ultimate fantasy, and that's why I never let him out of my sight for an instant.

SCORING:

1.	A=2	B=1	C=3
2.	A=1	B=3	C=2
3.	A=2	B=1	C=3
4.	A=3	B=1	C=2
5.	A=2	B=3	C=1
6.	A=1	B=3	C=2
7.	A=3	B=2	C=1
8.	A=2	B=3	C=1
9.	A=2	B=1	C=3
10.	A=3	B=2	C=1

THE VERDICT:

*If you scored between **10** and **17**:*

One thing's for sure—you're in no danger of being called a player. But if you ended up in this category, you've got other problems to deal with. When you're shutting yourself off from other people and letting things revolve completely around one guy, you run the risk of getting burned big-time. Not only will the rest of your world be hurting (your family and friends will feel abandoned, your schoolwork will go down the drain, etc.), but the relationship itself won't stand a chance. Nobody wants to be the center of someone else's existence—it's too much pressure, and it takes all the thrill out of being connected with someone who is, you know, *different* from you. So don't be afraid to put a little distance between you, and remember that you don't need to give up the rest of your life to be a loving, committed girlfriend.

If you scored between *18* and *23:*

You are the poster girl for healthy and well-balanced! When you're involved in a relationship, you take it—and your boyfriend—seriously. That means no lying, no sneaking around, and no cheating. You value what you've got without letting it take over your life. If your guy needs you, you're totally there for him. At the same time, you have no problem letting him know that other things are important to you also. You have the basis for a wonderful relationship.

If you scored between *24* and *30:*

You can't say you didn't see this guilty verdict coming. Your life is full of hopping from one guy to another. While Todd's arms are around you, your eyes are fixed on the guy in the corner. Dating around when you're not ready for something serious is totally acceptable—lying about it isn't. Being a player isn't about having lots of dates, it's about callously juggling people—and their feelings. Not only are you hurting them unfairly, but you're really cheating yourself as well. If you never pay enough attention to the person you're actually with, how will you know if he's what you've been looking for all along? Stop looking for Mr. Nonexistent Perfection and start focusing on what you really need to make you happy.

Do you ever wonder about falling in love? About members of the opposite sex? Do you need a little friendly advice but have no one to turn to? Well, that's where we come in . . . Jenny and Jake. Send us those questions you're dying to ask, and we'll give you the straight scoop on life and love.

DEAR JAKE

Q: *I've liked this guy, Rob, for a long time. Tom, who is friends with both of us, told me at first that Rob was interested too, and I should go for it. But now he says he was wrong, and he doesn't think Rob likes me after all. What can I believe?*

AW, New Port Richey, FL

A: Okay, so I know this girl Sally, and her friend Jane said Sally told her I was a total creep, but then *Erica* claimed that was such a lie, so now I'm asking Rebecca what she thinks. . . .

Get the picture? You're probably sitting there wondering why I don't just ask Sally herself what the deal is. The only way to get a straight answer is to go right to the source and ignore all third parties. Who knows where Tom is coming up with his information? Maybe he changed his story when he realized he was starting to like you a little too much and didn't want to encourage you in any direction but his.

Or maybe he's just completely guessing at everything. True, it's scary to talk to Rob directly and put yourself on the line like that, but when you're ready to know what's up, it's the only way you can be sure of finding out the truth.

DEAR JENNY

Q: *Eric is my friend's brother, and he and I have known each other for a long time. Recently he asked if I would go out with him, and I said yes. But now my friend is really mad at both of us. What do I do?*

NT, Radcliff, KY

A: It probably would have been a good idea for at least one of you—preferably *both* of you—to have checked it out with your friend before agreeing to go out with each other. She might be more upset by the feeling that you guys went behind her back than the fact that you're dating. Of course, technically it's only between you and Eric, but it's perfectly understandable that his sister would feel kind of hurt or left out, discovering that two people she's close to are sharing something separate from her.

This doesn't mean you and Eric can't still be together. What you have to do is talk about this—all three of you—until everyone is okay with the situation. Explain to your friend that whatever happens with you and Eric won't change how you both feel about her, and that you'll make sure she doesn't end up in the middle if there are ever any problems. These are most likely her biggest concerns. Once she's reassured, you and Eric can be free to be happy together.

Do you have questions about love? Write to:
Jenny Burgess or Jake Korman
c/o 17th Street Productions,
a division of Daniel Weiss Associates, Inc.
33 West 17th Street
New York, NY 10011

Don't miss any of the books in *Love Stories*
—the romantic series from Bantam Books!

You'll always remember your first love.

Love Stories

Looking for signs he's ready to fall in love?

Want the guy's point of view?

Then you should check out *Love Stories*. Romantic stories that tell it like it is—why he doesn't call, how to ask him out, when to say good-bye.

Love Stories

Available wherever books are sold.